PHANTOM
RAIDERS

PHANTOM RAIDERS

Western Stories

PETER DAWSON

Five Star • Waterville, Maine

First Edition
First Printing: April 2003

Published in 2003 in conjunction with
Golden West Literary Agency.

Set in 11 pt. Plantin by Al Chase.

Printed in the United States on permanent paper.

Library of Congress Cataloging-in-Publication Data

Dawson, Peter, 1907–
    Phantom raiders : western stories / by Peter Dawson.
    p. cm.
    Contents: Retribution River—Cutbank welcome—Signed
on Satan's payroll—The matched pair—Phantom raiders.
    ISBN 0-7862-3788-0 (hc : alk. paper)
    1. Western stories.   I. Title.
PS3507.A848 P48 2003
  813′.54—dc21
                                      2002068969

TABLE OF CONTENTS

Retribution River

Jonathan Glidden, who wrote as Peter Dawson, completed this story in mid-December, 1947. It was submitted by his agent to Jack Burr, editor of Street and Smith's *Western Story* shortly after the new year. Burr bought it for $187.50 at the rate of 2.5¢ a word. Five of the Peter Dawson novels had been previously serialized in this magazine when it was a weekly, and his short stories and short novels had been appearing in its pages for over a decade. This would prove to be the last Peter Dawson fiction to appear in *Western Story*, which since the March, 1944 issue had been a monthly magazine. The following July *Western Story* would publish its final issue, twenty years after it was launched in July, 1919, replacing Street and Smith's *New Buffalo Bill Weekly*. The author's title for this story was used when it appeared in the issue dated September, 1948, and it has been retained for its first book appearance.

I

Pete Sarran reined the badly blown buckskin into that last turning of Lost Man Trail and saw the river close ahead, while beyond it the black heights of the Buckhorns lifted into the nothingness of the night sky, their bulk ghostly yet welcoming in the light of a waning moon. Up there and beyond lay safety, something Pete was in need of tonight. When he was close enough to make out the ferry landing in the shadow of the cañon's straight wall, he breathed a long sigh of relief at seeing the barge against it and not on the far side. Presently, as the buckskin's hoof falls set up a hollow thunder against the ferry's planking, he was quick to put the animal alongside the windlass at the bow.

He wound the rope of the windlass arm around the saddle horn, starting the buckskin on a circle of the cable drum. The ferry moved slowly out from the bank, swaying against the pull of the current. White water boiled against the barge's side at midstream. It was beyond that point, as Pete reined the buckskin around to face the far bank, that he saw the bright orange eye of a lantern bobbing down the path from the ferryman's cabin.

"Kill the light, Avery!" he called loudly, and almost at once the gleaming dot lifted and went out.

The barge was grating over the gravelly shallows a full minute later when the ferryman's voice sounded sharply out of the blackness. "Careful! The cable's close to bustin'!"

Pete slowed the buckskin and in the gloom could finally make out Avery's stooped shape standing at the water's edge.

"New cable was due a month ago," the oldster growled. For a moment he watched Pete, flipping the windlass rope from the horn. Then, feelingly, solemnly, he said: "So now they're after you, Sarran."

Pete's head came around sharply. "How did you know?"

The barge jolted against the bank as Avery answered: "Heard it in town tonight. Besides, that's the law's nag you're forkin', son."

"So it is," Pete agreed. "But what was it you heard?"

"How Phil Cavendish lost some horses from his upper meadow last night. How he put his crew out on the sign today, and how they come across a brandin' fire up there near Owl Peak this afternoon."

Pete waited and, when the oldster didn't go on, queried: "What's all that got to do with me?"

"Y'don't know?"

"No."

"That no-good George Soule didn't tell you before you made off with his horse?"

"All he had a chance to say was that he had a warrant on me," Pete answered.

"That's all?"

Pete nodded. "Wasn't time for more. Soule got me out of bed, came in without being invited. By the time I got a lamp lit, a couple of Cavendish's hardcases were coming in the door after him. So I puffed at the light and got out of there without waitin' for particulars. Soule's horse was handiest, so I took him."

Avery sighed audibly. "The particulars don't listen too good. Cavendish's *segundo* brought Soule a hunk of mud he swore had been dug up near the ashes of that fire I mentioned. I saw the thing. There was the plain print on it of one of your Box S irons."

"So now I'm a rustler," Pete breathed, his thoughts running straighter than at any time over this past hour. "So here's where a man winds up when he bucks a range hog."

10

The oldster nodded. "Just where Sam Poole and Bob Saunders wound up."

A faint anger stirred in Pete. "No one's ever proved they rustled Cavendish's beef. And no one can hang this on me. Avery, I was in bed an hour after dark last night. If you think I drove those horses off, you're. . . ."

"Who the hell said I thought you did?" the ferryman cut in tartly. "Any more than I believe what they say about Sam and Bob. Would I be here wastin' breath on you if I had any love for Anvil?"

"No, you wouldn't," Pete admitted. He hadn't thought much about Avery in coming here, knowing only that once across the river he stood a good chance of getting out of the country. The ferryman was only a casual acquaintance, and his reaction to what was happening tonight came as something of a surprise to Pete.

"Give Cavendish another year and he'll own half the valley," Avery went on now. "Along with havin' most of the valley money in his new bank. Well, where you headed? Into the hills or beyond?"

"Beyond . . . 'way beyond," drawled Pete. "There's other land to file on as good as my lay-out. Besides, what good's one man against Anvil? And how do I know it was Cavendish that framed me?"

"Talk sense, man!" Len Avery flared. "It isn't only one man against Cavendish. There's Bob Saunders and Sam Poole."

The implication in these words jarred Pete, and, without thinking, he said: "Those two have been gone for over a year."

"So I hear," was the oldster's enigmatic reply. He cocked his head, turning riverward. "Well, do you drift or do you stay? Hear that? Better make up your mind in a hurry."

Pete did hear, and for several seconds stood listening to the faint yet strengthening drum of hoofs echoing down out of Lost Man. Several riders were coming along the trail to the river, and, unless he was mistaken, Pete knew who they were.

So finally he said: "If I wanted to find Sam and Bob, where would I start lookin'?"

"Come along," was Avery's abrupt answer. He turned back up the path that led to his cabin.

Leading the buckskin and following the ferryman, Pete for a few uncertain seconds doubted this hasty decision. But then the rancor brought on by all that had happened tonight boiled in him again to stiffen his resolve, and, by the time his lean length was moving toward the barn alongside Avery, he knew that he wasn't leaving the country as he'd planned when he rode in here.

Avery disappeared into the barn and presently came out leading a saddled black gelding. He was tightening the cinch when the sound of the running horses across the river abruptly strengthened. Then a voice across there was shouting something made unintelligible by the distance and the stream's steady racket.

"That'll be Soule," Avery grunted. "By the time they pull that rig across and get back again, we'll be out of their way."

"He'll wonder why you aren't here."

"Let 'im. I can tell him I was up on the meadow after trout. Fact is, think I'll take my pole along and try for a mess. That ought to tidy things up in case he comes nosin' around."

So they rode across to the cabin, and Avery went in to get a two-piece rod that he tied scabbard-fashion to his saddle. Shortly they took the steep hillside road away from the river. Before it dipped to block their view of the gorge, they looked back and made out the vague shadow of the ferry crawling away from the far bank, three riders silhouetted on it.

12

Halfway up the next long rise, Avery turned off the road along a rocky wash and, a hundred yards farther on, picked up the faint line of a trail Pete hadn't known was there. The roar of the river was gradually lost against the stillness until the only sounds were the hoof strikes of their ponies and the creak of their saddle gear.

The trail they were following presently slanted up a gentle rise through a stand of jack pine. A mile beyond, riding the edge of a gradually ascending rim, Avery broke the silence for the first time.

"You're wonderin' why I want to buy into your troubles, Sarran. Remember Stella Cavendish?"

"No. She must have been before my time."

Pete was trying to recall what he had heard of Phil Cavendish once having had a wife when Avery went on: "She was married to Cavendish a little under a year before he left her. That was across in Tombstone, before he made the killin' in cards that let him get his start here. Stella's happy now. She's married to another man. But that year was pure hell for her. She's my only child."

"I didn't know," Pete said gently.

"So it does matter to me what happens to Cavendish," the ferryman said solemnly. "I'd like to see someone knock him off his roost so hard it'd hurt."

"Chances are, you never will."

"You could be right," Avery muttered. For a time he was silent. Then: "He's got everything on his side. Soule, for instance. George Soule's honest enough, but he's got no brains. Cavendish every now and then reminds him of how it was on his say they let Soule run for office. Now George's got to thinking he owes Anvil something. Then take Cavendish's new bank. If his luck holds, the old one'll go broke inside another year."

"You've got to admit he's loaning money at easy rates," Pete said.

"Too easy! Today I had a talk with John Knight. Went in to see about a draft on a Denver bank to pay for that new cable. John claims he'd lose his doors if he made the kind of loans Cavendish has been makin'. Told me something else, too. Even for all the talk, the new bank has let out only two or three chunks of that easy money. Just enough to get people interested in switchin' their accounts. Knight says most of Cavendish's deals are hangin' fire."

"What's he after, then? To see Knight's bank go broke, then bleed folks for all he can get?"

"Something like that."

They fell silent again, for a time riding a timber-flanked trail too narrow for going side-by-side. Above that stretch, they headed up a winding stream along a steep-walled cañon.

"Suppose I do throw in with Bob and Sam," Pete wondered. "What can we do about Cavendish?"

"Don't worry about that. They've already thought up something. They haven't told me what it is, understand, but they're about ready for some sort of play. There's only one thing I don't like about it." Avery spoke now with unmistakable concern. "They've taken on a sidekick. Brazos, he calls himself. Unless I'm 'way wrong, he's a real dyed-in-the-wool hardcase."

"Maybe they need a man like that to go against Cavendish."

Avery gave an irritable lift of the shoulders. "We'll see," was all he said. Several moments later he was abruptly reining in, pointing toward the cañon's west wall. "This is as far as I side you. Wade that creek right on through that notch and you're there. Say howdy to the boys and tell 'em everything's set. They'll understand."

14

Looking yonder, Pete could see a narrow stream boiling down out of a notch in the sheer wall. The feeble light didn't give him much detail of the wall formation. He was studying it, trying to understand how a man could ride the stream's twisting course, when Avery added: "So long. Be seein' you in a day or two."

Pete had only time enough to say—"Much obliged, Avery."—before the ferryman unceremoniously rode out of hearing.

II

It was a full half minute before Pete touched the buckskin's flank with spur and rode on. Over that interval a strange uneasiness was gripping him, and he had the strong impulse to turn back down the cañon and ride away from whatever indefinable trouble he sensed was in the making. He was on his own now, completely so, faced for the second time with a choice, this one irrevocable.

The shadowed notch Avery had pointed out was the gateway to a life Pete had never thought he would be choosing, a life outside the law. He had only to turn and ride out of the cañon and across the hills to put all this behind him. In the end Pete put the buckskin straight at the notch, wading the stream squarely into it. As the shadows swallowed him until nothing but blackness lay ahead, he was feeling an odd excitement coupled with a vast relief. He had made his choice and it seemed right.

The going was slow, for time and again the buckskin stumbled over the tricky footing of the climbing streambed. Finally the animal plunged blindly through a dense thicket of alder choking the narrow space between the walls, and Pete had to lift an arm to keep the branches from slashing at his face.

Directly behind the thicket the walls fell suddenly away, and he was riding into the entrance to a broad grassy pocket clearly visible in the moonlight. The cobalt shadow of a belt of pines edged the upper end of the pocket some four hundred yards away, and Pete was looking off in that direction when a voice close to his right said sharply: "Stay where you are!"

Pete's glance whipped around to see a man's gaunt shape easing out from the shadow on the wall. His hands lifted to the level of his wide shoulders at sight of the carbine that was slanted at him. He asked: "Would Bob Saunders be around? Or Sam Poole?"

"What makes you think they would?" came the man's toneless query. Then, before Pete could answer: "Light! And slow, stranger!"

Carefully, moving his hands slowly, Pete came aground.

"Turn around," the man drawled, his tone uncompromising. When Pete had turned his back to him, the man came on in and thrust the carbine's muzzle hard against Pete's spine. Then, roughly, his free hand came around and jerked loose the Colt Pete was wearing in his belt.

Using the carbine as a prod, he pushed Pete away from him. "Now talk! Who sent you up here?"

"Avery," Pete said. "You must be this Brazos he told me about."

"The old fool runs off at the mouth," Brazos said. In the moonlight his narrow face showed a stony cast as he bluntly queried: "Who would you be?"

"Pete Sarran."

"Never heard the name."

"Bob and Sam have," Pete replied, keeping a tight rein on his rising temper.

"We'll see." Brazos motioned briefly with the carbine toward the upper end of the pocket. "Start walkin'."

Pete dropped the reins and started on up along the stream, looking behind to see that Brazos had mounted the buckskin and was following. Presently, as he neared the upward fringe of pines, Pete made out a pole corral in the shadows and then, beyond it, the squat shape of a cabin.

He was abreast the corral when Brazos called—"Far

17

enough. Stay set."—and rode around him.

Pete watched Brazos go in toward the cabin, and then lost sight of him. Standing there without moving for the better part of two minutes, he had the uneasy feeling that he was being watched and he didn't like what he had so far seen of Brazos.

All at once strong lamplight filled the rectangle of the cabin's doorway, and a moment later a stocky figure appeared there, calling: "Get in here, Pete!" Without waiting for Pete to appear, Bob Saunders came through the door toward him.

They were shaking hands when Sam Poole hurried out and joined them. Sam slapped Pete on the back, saying gladly: "Y'don't even have to tell us. You've tangled with Phil Cavendish or you wouldn't be here."

Pete nodded, sobered by the sight of Brazos leaning in the doorway, watching. Briefly he told them of what had happened that night. He was finishing, mentioning Avery's bringing him up here, when Brazos eased out from the doorway and, carbine slacked in the bend of his arm, sauntered out to join them.

"So he's all right?" Brazos questioned.

"Didn't we tell you he was?" Bob said. "Shake hands with one more gent that thinks Cavendish throws too big a shadow. He's with us from now on."

Neither Brazos nor Pete made any move to do as Bob suggested.

"Why don't we invite the whole town in on it?" Brazos said dryly.

"Now wait'll you get the straight of it before you go on the prod," Sam said quickly. "Pete's steady, and Cavendish has run him out pretty much the same as he did us. Why can't we use him?"

"Because three's enough for the job," was Brazos's cryptic answer.

"But four would be better," Bob put in. "Now don't worry about it, Brazos. Let's all go in and talk it over."

"You three do the talkin'. I'll get back down there," Brazos told him.

"Who'd be ridin' in here tonight?" Bob asked. "Forget it and hear what Pete has to say."

"*He* showed up, didn't he?" Brazos said pointedly. "If he could do it, another man could. I'll just get down there and make sure Avery hasn't invited someone else in."

They stood watching the outlaw walk away, and, when he was out of hearing, Bob said: "Never mind him, Pete. He's that way sometimes. If it wasn't for his ideas, we might get sore and do without him."

"What did he mean . . . 'three's enough for the job'?" Pete asked. "What job?"

They were close enough to the lighted doorway for Pete to see the wide smile that patterned Bob's square face.

"Do we tell him now?" Bob asked, looking at Sam.

"Now's as good a time as any."

Bob's glance slid around to Pete again. "It's the new bank, Pete."

"What about it?"

"Deposits are pourin' in there like wheat in a bin at threshin' time. We aim to do something about it."

"Rob it, you mean?" Pete asked, awed by the thought.

"Why not? Cavendish couldn't stand a loss like that. It's the one sure way of whittling him down to size. He'll be broke as a saddle tramp if it comes off right."

Pete's thoughts were confused, too jumbled to see the straight of the thing. All he could think of to say was: "Brazos thought this up?"

Both men nodded, and Sam observed: "He doesn't fool around with any penny-ante plays. He's handled giant powder before. Says blowin' in that vault will be easy."

"But he's not your kind," Pete insisted, clinging to his instinctive dislike of Brazos as the one tangible objection he could make to their plan. "You're a couple of top hands down on your luck, the same as me. He's a curly wolf, a killer maybe. What do we know about a play like this? Suppose something goes wrong and you have to fight your way out. You might have to cut down on one of your friends."

"We've talked that all out," Bob told him. "If we have to shoot, it'll be to cripple a man, not to kill him. Brazos is with us all the. . . ."

"Another thing," Pete cut in, a sudden urgency compelling him to further argument. "Maybe you'll be hurting Cavendish. But you'll be breaking a lot of other men along with him. Friends of yours can't afford to lose anything. Some mighty fine people have switched over to the new bank."

"Sure," Sam agreed easily. "We don't want the money. We find out who the losers are and pay them back on the quiet. All but Phil Cavendish."

Pete felt helpless now, incapable of further argument against their sure reasoning. He was groping for words when Bob said: "We've even fixed it with Avery for the getaway. At about ten tomorrow night he'll take a ratchet off the winch of the ferry and then, from his side, haul the ferry across to the other. No one can work it back without that ratchet. He'll hide the thing under a loose board by the drum. All we have to do is bolt the ratchet on again and cross over, takin' maybe ten seconds to get it to workin'. Once we're across, we're safe."

"And it'll be late enough so Avery can pretend he was

asleep and didn't hear us," Sam said. "Just in case anyone's on our tails and routs him out to question him."

Pete breathed a long sigh, shaking his head. He didn't like what he had heard, none of it. He could see how the plan might work, even how it would be possible to pay back the depositors who would suffer most from the robbery. Yet nothing seemed clear-cut in the shadow of his dislike for Brazos.

"What's wrong with it?" Bob asked now.

Pete shrugged. "I'd like it better if we were on our own."

Sam laughed softly. "I know how you feel. Same as I did about Brazos at first. He rubbed me the wrong way. But now I'm used to him. And don't think he won't pay off. He's cold as ice out of a mine shaft, don't give a hoot for anything but money. He's got no strings tied to him in this play like we have. He bosses the job, blows the safe, and we make our split. That's the last we see of him."

"He bosses it, you say?" Pete asked.

"Why shouldn't he? Like you said, this isn't our game. It's his. So he ramrods the thing and gets out after it's over. We pay a few calls some night, squarin' things with the people who've lost money. Then we sit back and watch Cavendish fold up."

Bob was eying Pete closely. "Well, how about it, feller?" he queried after a moment. "Are you with us?"

Pete didn't answer at once. He was weighing his doubts of Brazos against his liking for their obvious enthusiasm over the plan and the strong probability that they had found a sure way of striking back at Phil Cavendish. It was his feeling toward Cavendish that finally made him respond: "I'm with you." Knowing he would be hurting their chances if he made a halfway decision, he added: "With you all the way."

21

III

They rode a round-about trail reaching the river the very next evening, wading their horses across it ten miles above Avery's ferry crossing. By nine they were at the edge of town soberly listening as Brazos gave them their last instructions.

Brazos and Sam would go in along the alley, Sam to be look-out while Brazos was inside the bank working on the vault. Bob and Pete would be on the street, Bob holding his horse in a passageway below the bank toward the center of town, Pete watching from upstreet behind a thicket of locust saplings fronting the corner of a vacant lot.

After the explosion Pete and Bob were to stay in position until a signal, three closely spaced shots, told them that Brazos and Sam were on their way out. They would ride straight for the ferry, meet there, and make the crossing.

"Simple enough," Bob said when Brazos had finished.

"And remember," Pete couldn't help putting in, "if we throw lead, we're careful about it."

Brazos's thin face shaped a wry smile. "We've been over all that before," he said pointedly.

They separated then, Brazos and Sam riding off into the darkness while Pete and Bob started down toward the head of the street. The sting of Brazos's words stayed with Pete, and presently Bob showed that they had also had an effect on him, for he said in a low voice: "Forget him, Pete. By this time tomorrow he'll be long gone, and we'll have what we want."

"Maybe," Pete drawled, and they rode on in silence.

They separated at the outer end of the street, Pete taking to the street's shadowed aisle of cottonwoods, Bob heading on back for the alley. When Pete came abreast the vacant lot, he put the buckskin across the dirt walk, and then in behind the locust thicket, tying the animal there and coming back to stand on the path where the shadows were heaviest.

A long, studying glance down the street showed nothing to make Pete nervous, yet he was on edge, all his senses cocked to a strong wariness. Down at the livery he saw the hostler watering two teams that would be the relays for the ten o'clock stage. Window lights showed him plainly the usual idlers under the awning fronting the Four Corners. He noticed a light burning in the second-story window over Hill's Dry Goods and idly wondered what work kept lawyer Richardson at his desk so late.

Once Pete thought he glimpsed Sheriff George Soule's ramrod-straight shape easing across the side street beyond the bank, and alarm quickened his pulse, but the distance was too great for him to be sure, and he decided that, after all, it could have been another man. The minutes dragged on interminably. Twice he took out his watch and tried to read its face, but it was too dark to see.

He was looking at the watch a third time when a heavy thudding explosion cut loose, bringing a definite feel of concussion on the cool air against his face.

Instinctively he reached to the handle of the Colt at his belt. His palm was moist, and he wiped it along his thigh. He saw that the men on the walk in front of the Four Corners had turned to look across the street toward the bank. For long seconds no one down there moved.

Suddenly a shout rang along the street. Close on the heels of that sound a shot cut across the stillness, its deep echo slapping up between the false-fronted buildings. Someone screamed hoarsely, and Pete's frame went rigid as he realized that the cry came from the alley behind the bank.

A second gun's rosy wink of powder flame stabbed the

darkness to this side of the saloon, close to the passageway where Bob was supposed to be watching. Instantly a strong sense of foreboding settled through Pete.

Leaving the walk, he wheeled in behind the thicket, pulling loose the reins and leading the buckskin out into the street. Down there now he could see men running across from the Four Corners toward the bank. A hoof pound abruptly sounded from the opposite alley, strengthening fast as it came toward him. He was keenly aware that it was only one horse on the run, and, as the sound drew abreast of him, then ran on past, he peered into the shadows across the street between two houses, vainly hoping to glimpse the rider.

The rhythmic clatter of that hard-running horse died fast, and Pete looked down the street again, catching his breath at what he saw. A knot of men had gathered along the walk at the head of the passageway where Bob had been watching. Three others were running this way, and Pete was in time to see them turn in at the livery barn. Suddenly the full realization came that something had gone wrong, and he knew that time was running out for him, that the hunt would soon be on.

He swung quickly up into the saddle. Yet some vague fear and the thought that either Bob or Sam needed him now kept him from riding away. Only when the three men at the barn reappeared, leading half a dozen saddled horses, did he rein the buckskin around and head out the street at a walk. At the edge of town his restlessness and his need for knowing what had happened made him lift the animal to a run, hoping to overtake the lone rider who, a few minutes ago, had ridden so fast from town.

Half a dozen times on that two-mile ride to the river Pete stopped to listen. But no sound reached him over the river's distant and restless voice. When he finally sighted the stream

24

at the foot of Lost Man, he went on faster, studying the shadows that lay around the ferry landing.

No one was there waiting for him.

Moving quickly, Pete put the buckskin onto the barge, and then pulled aside the loose board Bob had so carefully described to him. When he had finished bolting on the ratchet, there came a sudden let-down. He had nothing to do now but wait—and wonder what could have happened to the rider, either Sam or Brazos, who had left town ahead of him and ridden this way. The first five minutes passed slowly. After that a growing impatience added to his worry until finally he left the barge and began restlessly pacing the riverbank.

A sound suddenly rose over the river's steady murmur, riding down out of Lost Man. For long moments Pete stood rigid, trying to read it. All at once, he wheeled and ran onto the barge, knowing that this was going to be close. Horses were coming down the trail, more than the three men—Bob, Sam, and Brazos—would be riding.

He was just beyond midstream, working the buckskin hard at the windlass, when the sound of the oncoming riders abruptly strengthened and he knew they were rounding the final bend on the river. He tightened the buckskin's circle around the windlass and began using the spur, wondering if the shadow of the cañon's east wall would block out the light of the moon enough to keep them from sighting him.

Hardly had the thought come to him when a rifle's brittle bark slapped across the water at him. A moment later one of the rail boards *thumped* at a bullet's impact. Looking back, Pete could see vague shadows moving about near the cable post. As he watched, two gun flashes winked brightly at him, and an instant later he felt the air whip of a bullet strike the side of his face.

Feeling the barge sliding over the shallows, he tossed aside the windlass rope and jumped the buckskin from the end of the barge into the knee-deep water, running the animal for the bank. Then he was clear of the water, the hollow bark of the guns following him up the steep trail to where Avery's cabin stood.

He was almost abreast the cabin when he saw a man's shape standing there on the trail ahead of him. His right hand edged toward his Colt before he recognized Avery and pulled the buckskin to a quick halt.

"So your luck ran out," came the ferryman's sober words.

"Unless the others have come through ahead of me."

Avery shook his head. "No." He paused momentarily, then went on. "Half a mile above you'll come to a lightning-struck pine. Swing hard left beyond it and follow out that cut. At the end of it you can begin a circle back here. If it's safe for you to come on in, the place'll be dark. Stay away if you see a light. Now get goin' and I'll handle 'em."

The guns across the river had gone quiet now, for the trail had climbed beyond sight of the posse. Pete ran the buckskin up the first long grade and, at its crest, drew in long enough to look down on the river. Avery was just starting across, his lantern a bright pinpoint against the blackness. Pete could faintly hear the shouts of the men on the far bank, and once made out Avery's voice replying.

When, after several minutes of steady going, Pete came to the lightning-blasted pine, he realized that Avery must have carefully thought out this very possibility. For the stretch of trail beyond the pine's tall branchless spear was rocky and rough, too barren for the leaving of any sign that could have told a tracker where an animal had left the trail.

Once below, along the wash, the small panic that had been in Pete quieted enough to let him think things out. By the

26

time he had ridden out the length of the cut and was swinging back riverward again, he had come to a grim and stubborn resolve.

Some twenty minutes later when he brought the cabin into sight, he was careful to keep to the shadows of the trees and study what lay ahead. The cabin was dark, Avery's signal that it was safe to come on in. Still Pete stayed where he was for better than five minutes, standing with hand ready if the buckskin threatened to whicker.

At the end of that long interval his probing glance caught a hint of movement along the cabin's riverward wall. Gradually he made out a figure standing there but wasn't at all sure who it might be. Not until Len Avery struck a match and lit his pipe a couple of minutes later did Pete go on, leading the buckskin.

Avery heard Pete coming and sauntered out to meet him.

"Sarran, you'd better keep right on goin'," he said at once. "As far and as fast as you can. George Soule had a look at his nag's sign across there and knows it's you. He's sore enough to chew nails. Says there'll be a reward on you by mornin'. He's taken the rest on to block the pass trails."

"What went wrong?" Pete asked tonelessly.

"Everything! Sam got a hunk of lead through the shoulder and is hurt bad. Soule himself took Saunders. They're both locked up."

"And Brazos?"

"Got clean away. As near as they can tell, there's fifty thousand gone from the vault in big notes. That payroll was part of it. Now we'll watch Phil Cavendish sweat." There was a strong note of satisfaction in Avery's voice.

Pete ignored that. "What payroll?"

"One that came in last this afternoon by stage. Soule got to

27

worryin' about it, which is how he come to be prowlin' around and had spotted Bob there in that passageway alongside the bake shop just before the blast cut loose. All he had to do was go around the building and take Bob from behind. Then. . . ."

"What went wrong out back . . . with Sam?" Pete cut in, sure he was close to discovering something significant.

He caught Avery's frown as the ferryman said: "They couldn't figure that out. Far as anyone could tell, no one was out behind the bank until after Brazos made his getaway."

"And Brazos didn't come this way," Pete drawled in a chill voice. "Which means he never aimed to."

Avery studied him closely in the faint light. "What're you tryin' to say, Sarran?" he asked at last.

"That Brazos shot Sam. That he planned a double-cross from the beginning."

Avery gave a visible start. "You're wrong. Things just didn't go right and. . . ." The ferryman's words broke off abruptly and an awed look crossed his thin face as he breathed. "By Satan, it could be!"

"I heard him head out of town. Toward the ferry road," Pete said quietly. "He'd cut Sam down and he had the money. His easiest way out of the country was across here. Yet he didn't take it. Which means he sold us out."

Avery breathed a long restless sigh. "It'll go hard with Sam and Bob. But. . . ." He shrugged. "Anyway, Cavendish'll be dancin' on a mighty hot griddle. That much is good."

"And the rest bad," Pete intoned. "Bob and Sam locked up, probably headed for trial. The new bank busted and all those people broke along with it." He shook his head. "It just can't happen, Avery."

"How you goin' to keep it from happening?" was Avery's pointed question.

Pete thought a long moment, taking a sack of tobacco from shirt pocket and idly beginning to roll a smoke before he answered: "Go back across there and see what happened to Brazos. Follow him. Run him down if it takes a month . . . or a year. Maybe get the money and bring it back here to help these people."

"Maybe," the ferryman echoed acidly. "And maybe not. Hell, man, every peace officer from here to the Canadian will be on the look-out for you! Sooner or later one of them will collect that reward. Then where'll you be?"

"Where would I be if I just plain rode out on this thing now, Avery?"

"Alive, anyway."

Pete gave a slow shake of the head. "And never forgettin' that I had a part in breaking this range. No, I'll play it my way, friend. You can take me back across the river. Now."

IV

It was at the first gray light of dawn, with the pattern of the ground barely discernable, that Pete picked up the tracks of Brazos's horse barely a hundred yards out from the end of the alley at the town's edge. An hour ago he had been on the hill close above where Bob and he, Sam and Brazos had last night parted company before riding on down and into Arrowhead.

By the shielded light of a match Pete had studied the two sets of tracks made by Brazos's and Sam's animals. The set here at the alley's end was one of that pair, obviously made by Brazos in his getaway.

The light was still too poor for Pete to see the ground from the saddle. So he started walking along the line of the tracks, knowing he was running the risk of being seen. Yet it was worth the gamble, this chance he had of discovering which way Brazos had gone last night.

He had walked nearly a quarter of a mile, and Brazos's sign was swinging gradually northward, away from the Lost Man Trail, when finally the light strengthened enough to let Pete mount Soule's buckskin and work along faster.

By the time the first bright sunlight touched the peaks far across the river, Pete was well above town in the hills and following Brazos's tracks that had made a complete half circle and were headed east, away from the river. Arrowhead was below in the valley now. So here, definitely for the first time, was evidence that the outlaw had acted contrary to the plan of meeting at the ferry.

Over the next two hours, Pete covered only four miles. At times he had to dismount and hunt out the sign when the going became rocky or ran through the maze of thickets in the

30

higher timber. Finally, at the end of those two hours, he was decidedly puzzled. The sign was leading him straight up a broad cañon he knew became a box at the base of a thousand-foot rim. By the time he had passed the last offshoot that led from the cañon, with the walls abruptly climbing and the cañon's width narrowing, a strong wariness was in him.

Deep in a tangle of jack pine and scrub oak flanking a stream he stopped and carefully cast back, trying to remember every detail of this upper end of the box. Almost a mile above was a long, narrow meadow centered by this creek where a nester had two years ago tried to run a band of sheep before the cattlemen ran him out. At the head of that meadow laid an abandoned line shack, its single window gone and its rear half capsized where a windfall had fallen across its roof. Close above the shack, closer than a quarter mile, lay the end of the box, its enclosing walls too sheer to be climbed by either animal or man.

Pete saw that he had no choice here. Close below, just now, he had lost Brazos's sign and ranged the whole width of the cañon before picking it up again. He hadn't come across other tracks, so he could be sure the outlaw hadn't ridden out, and, considering what lay ahead, Pete knew that it would be foolhardy to go any farther. Yet he must find out what had happened to Brazos.

In the end, he turned around and rode the better part of half a mile, until he reached a trail that climbed to the west rim. Halfway up the trail he was thankful for the timber that screened him. Higher, he punished the buckskin and put the animal across the last hundred yards of the trail as fast as he would go, not feeling safe until he was on the rim and well back from it.

Going on, following out the line of the cañon, he rode to the rim as infrequently as possible, coming aground each time and picking cover that kept him from being silhouetted from below. Each of these times he spent several minutes carefully studying what lay below, not wanting to give Brazos the chance of riding out without being seen.

Finally he saw the long meadow and made out the cabin at its head. He didn't return to the rim again until the cabin lay almost below and he had tied the buckskin well back from the drop-off.

Pete's first glimpse of the shack showed him no more than the countless others he had taken throughout the day. Along toward noon he became impatient and walked several hundred rods, until he was well above the shack, then looked down from there. But from this angle the tall lodgepole pines obscured most of the shack, spoiling his hope that he could see in through its ruined rear.

He came back to the buckskin and took out some biscuits and jerky Avery had given him and ate a cold meal. After that, he became as thirsty as he was impatient. But he didn't leave the rim to ride the mile to a small spring he had passed on the way up here.

He's down there, he had to keep telling himself as the late afternoon shadows gathered in the cañon below him, and it was hard to believe his own words. Many times he thought back on every detail of his ride up the cañon this morning, trying to see where he could have made the mistake that would mean he had wasted a day watching an empty shack. But when he had thought it all through, he couldn't see any possibility of Brazos's not being down there.

As the first hint of twilight set in, the sun dipping below the Buckhorns, Pete was longing for a Winchester, wondering if he could accomplish anything with his .45. If Brazos was in the shack, he was being inordinately careful—so careful that it would take a bullet to bring him out.

Pete was thinking this, had even taken the Colt from his belt and was looking down at it, wondering if he should use it, when a stray sound echoed up from below. It sent him belly-down, wide hat laid aside, peering downward into the thickening shadows. He watched for two minutes, another, without seeing anything, time and again blinking his eyes to sharpen his vision.

Then all at once he saw the rider coming up along the meadow's edge headed straight toward the shack. It took him only an instant to recognize that tall, portly figure in the saddle. It was Phil Cavendish!

Suspicion came alive in Pete to become a certainty in an alarmingly short space of time. Hardly had he taken in the fact that something unusual was bringing Anvil's owner to this out-of-the-way spot than Cavendish was drawing rein in front of the shack and swinging aground. In that moment a slat-bellied figure appeared in the shack's doorway. It was Brazos.

Pete watched them shake hands, soberly and deliberately meditating upon the meaning of their meeting. Slowly a cold rage was building in him, an emotion tinged with a nameless foreboding that was almost fear. He wanted, more than he had ever wanted anything, to be down there within gunshot range of the shack.

His thinking ran straight and clear when, seeing Brazos go back into the shack to appear shortly leading his horse, he realized that they were headed out. He crawled back from the rim and, beyond their sight, ran back to the buckskin to swing up into the saddle. He started back from the rim and, at a quarter mile distance from it, spurred the animal to a lope.

V

Darkness was nearly complete when, better than half an hour later, Pete reached the head of the trail leading down into the cañon. He was thankful for that mantle of blackness as he put the buckskin down off the rim. He felt sure he was ahead of Cavendish and Brazos, for he had ridden hard and they would be in no special hurry. He considered the possibility of their coming up this trail when they reached it, but put the idea aside in the knowledge that behind the rim lay nothing but a tangle of hills and cañons leading nowhere.

So he rode on downcañon and in ten more minutes found a spot that suited his purpose. Here the cañon narrowed, alder and willow thickets choking its width except for the opening the stream ran through. In one place the water ran alongside a ten foot high boulder to form a deep pool. A long rapids close above gave out a steady rush of sound, a fact that eased Pete's worry now about tying the buckskin deep in the willows behind the boulder, for the animal wouldn't be able to hear the approach of other horses and signal them.

When Pete had hunkered down on a narrow ledge near the top of the boulder directly above the pool, he was satisfied. Even in the starlight he could make out each clear detail of the thicket across from him. Nothing could pass between this boulder and that thicket without his seeing it.

He wasn't expecting it to happen so soon. He had barely settled himself comfortably on the ledge when the hollow striking of a shod hoof against rock struck out its clear warning. His hand stabbed to his belt and drew the Colt. He saw the rider coming toward him then, barely twenty feet away and wading the far margin of the stream. He could easily recognize the man as Brazos.

Instantly alarm struck through him and he was asking himself why Brazos rode alone. But he had no time even to guess at an answer, for the outlaw was drawing abreast and in scant seconds would be gone.

Pete eased erect and leveled the Colt. "Brazos!" he called loudly.

His word visibly struck the outlaw. Brazos's head jerked around. He stiffened and instinctively drew rein. His animal came to a nervous stand as Pete called out again: "Drop your belt, Brazos!"

Pete was looking over the sights as the outlaw, moving his left hand carefully, unbuckled his heavy shell belt and swung it out, dropping it in the brush along the edge of the far bank.

"Now come across," Pete told him, easing the Colt down yet keeping thumb on hammer.

Brazos waded his horse through the pool, his boots dragging the water. The horse lunged up the bank and, facing the thick green of willows, stopped abruptly.

Pete slid down off the boulder, shouldering through the willows until he stood below Brazos, looking up at him. He was about to speak when he caught the buckskin's uneasy whicker from deeper in the thicket. But he forgot that immediately, deciding the animal had heard Brazos's horse.

"So Cavendish had you rob his bank," he drawled, the words a statement rather than a query.

He didn't understand the flinty set of the outlaw's features, nor his cocksure tone as he replied: "Sure. Not a bad way to rig it, eh?"

A sudden uneasiness ran through Pete. "Where's Cavendish?"

In the faint starlight, he could make out the slow smile that came to Brazos's gaunt face. Then the outlaw was saying: "Right behind you."

Pete's involuntary turn was half complete when a hard object rammed his spine.

"Hold it!" Phil Cavendish's voice said sharply.

For the space of a second Pete considered his chances. Then, knowing he didn't have any, he opened his hand and dropped the .45.

It was typical of Anvil's owner that he found something amusing in the situation, for he laughed softly now as he said: "A nice try, Sarran. But not nice enough. You forgot one thing. I spotted your sign on the way in. This seemed a good place for you to make your play, so we baited you."

Those galling words drove home to Pete the utter finality of his predicament. He knew with an absolute certainty that his last chance was gone, that neither Cavendish nor Brazos would have any mercy on him now. They had too much at stake to risk anything. A short double-barreled Greener in the Anvil owner's hand added to that conviction.

Brazos wheeled his horse and rode back across the stream to lean down and recover his belt and holstered Colt from the far bank. Cavendish came around Pete and picked up his weapon.

"You should've listened to your jughead, Sarran," Cavendish said. "He tried to tell you I was coming up on you." He prodded Pete once more in the back with the shotgun, adding: "Get on over to him and we'll be movin'."

Pete pushed his way into the tangle of the willows, for a moment holding a slender hope that here was a chance to break away. But the threat of the Greener, probably loaded with buckshot, quickly restored his sanity and cautioned him to make no move Cavendish could misread.

Once Pete was in the saddle, Cavendish said—"Straight

on through."—and Pete pushed the buckskin deeper into the willows, looking down once to see that Cavendish was walking just behind his stirrup. From behind came the rustle of Brazos's horse as he made his way through the thicket after them.

The Anvil owner's mount was tied at the back edge of the thicket close to the climbing wall of rock. Without a word, Cavendish swung up into leather and motioned Pete on with the shotgun. Pete in the lead, the other two close behind, they pushed on out of the willows and into the open. There, Cavendish closed in until his horse's head was abreast Pete's stirrup. Presently the Anvil man said: "You had your warning two nights ago, Sarran. Why in blazes didn't you drift?"

"Now I wish I had," Pete drawled, knowing it was useless to show his real feelings.

"You're leaving me no choice on what to do with you," Cavendish told him with pointed meaning.

The impulse to know the details of the man's treachery all at once struck Pete and the next moment he was saying: "You had a choice with Bob and Sam. Why did you rope *them* in on this?"

"They were in my way, the same as you. Sooner or later I'd have had to deal with them. Getting rid of them now seemed simplest," came the man's bland admission.

"Just how were we in your way?" Pete couldn't keep the anger out of his tone as he looked around.

Cavendish smiled thinly. "It's my hope that Anvil's fence will one day cross the whole slope from Lost Man to Beaver Creek," he said. "Saunders and Poole wouldn't sell to me, neither would you. So. . . ." His deliberate lift of the shoulders was more eloquent than any words could have been.

"So you had your own bank robbed," Pete said. "How does that get you the slope?"

"It doesn't. Not just now, at any rate. We'll have to close the bank and pay off, say thirty cents on the dollar. I'll make some fairly generous offers on certain outfits I want . . . Baxter's and Lamb's, for instance. Then I can do my best to help a few unfortunates who lost heavily, make them loans. It's a fifty-fifty bet they'll never be able to pay off."

"So in a couple of years you get those outfits, too?"

Cavendish shrugged. "Maybe two years, maybe five. It makes little difference." He nodded on ahead. "Well, here's where I leave you."

They were low along the cañon now, and, looking ahead, Pete saw that the definite line of a trail angled west through the scattered, low-growing juniper and lined toward a notch in the rim, six or seven miles beyond which lay the upper head of Lost Man.

"This'll do," Cavendish said as they came up on the trail. In several moments, as they stood their horses, Brazos joined them.

"Sarran is going with you," Phil Cavendish told the outlaw.

"That wasn't part of the deal," Brazos said dryly.

"No, it wasn't. But the day they find Sarran, I'm sending you a thousand dollars by express. That suit you?" At Brazos's brief nod, Cavendish went on: "Spend your money any way you want, but don't talk. Drift back here next spring and I'll have something more for you to do. Some of these people may be hard to persuade." He added significantly: "If you talk, you're losing some more easy money. And if you do talk, don't think you'll be hurting me. No one would believe what you had to say."

"Who said I was talkin'?" Brazos asked angrily.

"No one. Only it's better that these things be understood now rather than regretted later." Cavendish reined away, lifting a hand. *"Adiós."*

38

It was Brazos half a minute later, as the Anvil owner rode out of sight down the cañon, who worded what both he and Pete were thinking when he said: "There's as cool a customer as you'll ever run into. And I've come across some that snow wouldn't melt in their innards. Well, let's go."

Pete made no move to lift rein, and Brazos, peering hard at him, reached down finally and drew his Colt from holster, lining it. "I said let's go."

"You'll kill a man for a thousand dollars?" Pete asked tonelessly. "I'll pay you that much to let me go."

He could faintly make out that Brazos was smiling as the outlaw gave a slow shake of the head. "Brother, a thousand is only part of it." Brazos reached behind him with his rein hand, slapping the roll of his cantle. "There's fifteen thousand in cash wrapped up right here. You heard what Cavendish said. Next spring there'll be more. You think I'd sell out a good thing like this for a thousand? Uhn-uh! Now get that nag of yours movin', friend, or I let this thing off right here!"

VI

All the way across the Lost Man, Pete had tried to think of a way out of this and, riding down the gulch, had several times tried to reason with the outlaw. But Brazos had so completely ignored him after his first attempt that Pete might as well have been talking to a Sioux who understood nothing of the language.

So now as they rode down on the river, a tense silence between them, Pete was thinking of Len Avery, wondering if he could attract the ferryman's attention, once they had reached the far bank, and in some way get his help.

As though reading his thoughts, Brazos abruptly spoke: "No one's goin' to bother us here. Avery's in town tonight, accordin' to Cavendish. A new cable for this rig of his arrived this afternoon and he's haulin' it out in the mornin'."

With that blasting of his last hope, Pete rode onto the barge and followed the outlaw's order that he should work the windlass. He started the buckskin on the monotonous round of drawing the winch bar, and, as the barge crept slowly out into the stream, a strong anger and rebellion against giving up so easily was gripping him. He knew that Brazos wouldn't wait long after reaching the far bank to carry out his grisly task. It now finally came to him that he had nothing to lose in trying a getaway since he was to cash in anyway.

The first impulse that struck him was to jump from the saddle over the rail and take his chances on swimming the river. But a brief glance at Brazos showed him the man sitting his horse close by, right hand holding his drawn Colt and that arm resting idly on the horn of the saddle. Brazos had only to lift the weapon and Pete was dead, probably before he hit the water.

He got to thinking of Avery then, wondering why his luck had so turned against him that he was being robbed of even the slim chance of getting the ferryman's help. Avery's new cable, long delayed, *would* have to arrive tonight and take him away from his cabin at the precise time Pete needed him. Why couldn't Avery have waited until morning to go in for the cable? Did the small span of the hours between tonight and tomorrow morning mean so much where the new cable was concerned? Was Avery afraid it would give way overnight or . . . it might!

Suddenly remembering how worried Avery had been about the cable night before last laid that lightning stab of hope through Pete. At once a high excitement ran through him, its intensity making him tremble. He didn't wait to analyze his chances, knowing only that there was a chance and that he had to take it. He rode the buckskin on around the slow circle, came face to face with Brazos, then abreast him. He lifted his boot clear of stirrup and, keenly aware of Brazos only ten feet away, kicked hard at the windlass' reversing lever.

The barge was riding the edge of swift water, the cable taut against the heavy load. The windlass locked as the lever swung over, and the barge jolted as solidly as though grounding on a boulder. The buckskin staggered, lost footing, and went to his knees. Pete, throwing himself to the side, fell toward the planks as Brazos's .45 thundered.

As his shoulder hit and he rolled over, Pete saw Brazos falling toward him. The outlaw had momentarily forgotten his weapon and was reaching out blindly in an effort to break his fall, his horse still on his feet but lunging from under him. Pete came to his knees and, as Brazos struck the deck, dove in at him.

At the instant he came down solidly on top of the outlaw, Pete felt the cable snap to tilt the barge in a sudden, violent lurch. Then he was crying out in pain as one of Brazos's spurs raked his right shin. He raised a fist and drove it at the outlaw's face, but at the last moment Brazos ducked and the fist only grazed his cheek bone.

Pete felt rather than saw the upward swing of the outlaw's gun arm and he struck out blindly, the Colt exploding deafeningly as his wrist struck the arm. He saw the weapon spin out of Brazos's grasp, then the man was thrashing from under him, and he was rolling onto his feet.

He came erect a split second before Brazos straightened and put all the strength of his heavy shoulders behind the full swung he aimed for the man's jaw. The barge lurched again, and Brazos cried out in fear an instant before Pete's blow lifted him fully erect. Pete swung once more and connected, and Brazos staggered on back into his horse before he toppled forward, unconscious.

Now, abruptly, Pete was for the first time aware of the barge tilting violently from side to side. He looked toward the town side of the river to see the rock cañon wall racing past but coming in on the barge with a speed that made him catch his breath. The cable had parted at a point beyond the barge toward Avery's side of the stream, and the locked windlass was bringing the ferry in to the town side, still held by the unbroken length of cable.

All Pete could think of to do as that wall of rock loomed quickly in at him was to go to his knees and wait. Two seconds later he was knocked flat by the barge's impact against the rocky bank. Brazos's horse, going down, kicked wildly, and a hoof grazed Pete's shoulder in a numbing blow. The outlaw's limp shape skidded toward him ten feet along the planks, and the buckskin was knocked into the windlass but managed to stay on his feet. Spray boiled over the barge's bow, its icy chill bringing Pete to his feet again. Then, miraculously, the barge settled solidly on the rocks.

Pete dragged Brazos to the rail and lifted him over, dropping him onto a steep talus slope that slanted into the stream. He managed to catch the reins of the outlaw's horse and quiet him. The buckskin was more manageable as Pete led both animals to the upstream end of the ferry. He tied them there and went back to pick up Brazos's Colt. Then, back by the horses again, he gingerly lowered himself over the bow into the water, reaching for bottom.

The water was swirling at his waist just above the belt when his boots touched rock. He waded ashore and then around to Brazos. Lifting the outlaw by a hold at his armpits, he dragged him on around to the bow of the barge and then into the water, abruptly dropping him.

Brazos regained consciousness as his head went under, and he beat out wildly with arms and legs until Pete lifted him to his feet. Pete stepped back from him then, letting his long frame ease down until he sat on the crumbled talus at the stream's edge.

"Now, friend," he drawled, "you're going to get those horses off there and over here where it's safe. Then we ride for town."

VII

Phil Cavendish reached Arrowhead at a few minutes past eight and went directly to the hotel for a late meal. He was interrupted several times in his eating by serious-faced men who came over to his table wanting to know what the bank's prospects were. He answered the last man as patiently as he had the first, and in practically the same words: "Fred, honestly I don't know. As soon as we've finished an audit, we'll see. I'm sorry as can be about the thing. But if you go broke, I'll be right with you. Every spare dollar to my name was in the vault."

He was letting his second cup of coffee cool when he saw Len Avery appear in the lobby doorway. The old ferryman scanned the room quickly, saw Cavendish, and came straight on across to his table. "George Soule wants to see you at his office," Avery announced unceremoniously. "Right away."

Cavendish frowned, inwardly uneasy. It was a rare thing for his former father-in-law even to speak to him when they met on the street, let alone address him out of choice. Yet he took a certain pride in hiding his feelings and now simply nodded and came up out of his chair, tossing a silver dollar onto the table. As he joined Avery and they crossed the lobby, he queried casually: "Something important?"

"You can decide that for yourself," was the ferryman's noncommittal answer.

All the way up the street and across it, Cavendish's curiosity was strengthening. Over his wonderment he tried to make small talk, first about the weather, then about the robbery, finally inquiring as to Avery's most recent word from his daughter. Only this last elicited more than a grunt.

"Stella's just the same as dead and gone, far as you're con-

44

cerned. She never asks about you, so you'd better not about her."

"Now, Len," the Anvil owner said smoothly, a touch of mockery in his tone, "you know I'm interested in Stella."

Avery trudged on in silence, making no comment, and shortly they were coming up on the sheriff's office. Cavendish noticed at once that the blinds on the two front windows were drawn.

He was almost abreast the door when he happened to glance out to the tie rail beyond and see George Soule's buckskin standing there. Sight of the animal made him halt suddenly.

"That's Soule's horse," he said sharply. "Where'd he come from?"

"Maybe you'd better let George tell you," came Avery's level reply.

There was a moment in which Cavendish was tempted to turn around and leave Avery, for he sensed that something had possibly gone wrong with his plans. Yet in the end he knew that, whatever surprise awaited him in the sheriff's office, now was no time to show his uneasiness. So he followed Avery to the door.

Avery lifted the latch and pushed the door open, stepping aside to let Cavendish go through first. Schooling his expression to impassiveness, Cavendish went on in. Yet he was only a step across the threshold when he stopped suddenly, as though he had run into a wall.

George Soule sat at his desk, stiff in his swivel chair. At the back edge of the desk, well out of his reach, lay his shell belt and .44 Colt. Alongside that edge stood Bob Saunders. Beyond him Sam Poole, pale-faced and his right arm hung in a flour-sacking sling, sat in a rickety leather-upholstered chair.

Yet it was the sight of the two others in the room's front corner that had stopped Cavendish. Brazos sat on a wall bench, elbows on knees and head down. Pete Sarran stood in the corner close to the outlaw, idly leaning against the wall with a Colt hanging in his hand.

Cavendish heard the door close and behind him caught the scrape of Avery's boots moving aside. Those sounds somehow quieted the near panic in him so that he was able to meet Soule's questioning look and ask evenly: "What's on your mind, George?"

The sheriff sent a helpless glance in Pete's direction. "Damned if I know!" he blurted out. "Sarran barges in here with this stranger and lays a gun on me. Claims this ranny's the man that got away with the bank's money last night."

"He damn' well is the one," Bob Saunders put in. "He. . . ."

Soule's fist banged the desk. "You're the county's prisoner and you'll let me handle this!" he exploded. He looked up at Cavendish again. "Phil, would you know any of that missing money if you saw it?"

"Maybe."

The lawman reached into the open the top drawer of his desk, lifting out two packets of banknotes bound in bright green strips of paper along with a small buckskin bag that clinked metallically as he set it on the desk. "Recognize it?"

Cavendish stepped over to the desk, picked up first the banknotes, then the bag. "What's in this?" he asked finally.

"Double eagles," the sheriff replied.

Cavendish returned the gold to the desk, shaking his head. "The notes might be anybody's. But the gold certainly isn't ours. We haven't seen that many double eagles since we opened our doors."

Brazos stirred now, rising up off the bench. "That satisfy

you, Sheriff?" he asked tersely. "I'll tell you once more. I'm down from Montana buying feeders. Maybe it was a fool notion to carry all this money with me. But it's mine and I'll swear out a warrant on this man for jumpin' me and draggin' me in here." As he spoke, he had turned to half face Pete.

Pete's glance ran on past Brazos now to settle on Cavendish. "This man and Cavendish were together less than two hours ago, Soule," he said quietly. "They. . . ."

"I know," the lawman cut in wearily. "Phil had hired this stranger to play along with Saunders and Poole on that hold-up, then double-cross 'em. You were one of their bunch, which is as much as I believe. The rest is as tall a tale as I've ever listened to. Imagine," he snorted, "Sarran havin' the gall to claim you stuck up your own bank, Phil!"

The lawman started laughing, and for several seconds the sound of his voice filled the room. But then, as he ran out of breath and went quiet, Len Avery said softly: "Sarran's tellin' the truth. And I can prove it."

Every eye in the room swung toward the oldster. Pete reached out and roughly pulled Brazos down onto the bench once more, lifting his Colt in a brief gesture that cut short a protest from the outlaw.

"Cavendish, remember sending me word last week that you were bringin' those steers down the mountain and would want to use the ferry most of one day?" Avery questioned.

Cavendish frowned momentarily, then nodded.

"What day was it to be?" Avery asked.

"Tomorrow," answered Cavendish.

"Correct," Avery said. "Now this afternoon I got word that the new cable for my rig arrived. The old one's been dangerous, and, in fact, it busted with Sarran tonight. Anyway, I decided to spend tomorrow hangin' the new cable. So, rememberin' you'd planned on using the ferry tomorrow, I rode out to Anvil late this afternoon to tell you to hold up for a day or so. About half a mile short of the lay-out I spotted you ridin' off into the hills to the west." He was eying Cavendish sharply now. "Get what I'm aimin' at?"

Cavendish's expression was impassive as he said: "No, I don't."

"You will. Why I tried to catch you instead of ridin' in and leavin' word with someone else, I'll never know. But that's what happened. You were in a hurry, and I never like to ride so fast. So I just hung along your back trail. Until. . . ." Here Avery paused to lend emphasis to his words. "Until you turned up that cañon where that Tejano tried to run those sheep summer before last."

As Avery finished and several moments of silence ran on, George Soule's puzzled glance was studying Cavendish. "That's funny," he said at length. "Ties in with Sarran's story, too." His tone was apologetic as he next put a question: "How about it, Phil?"

Cavendish nodded readily enough. "Yes, all that's true. I was up that cañon today."

"Now tell us why," Pete drawled.

Cavendish gave him a cool, appraising glance. "Why should I be obliged to tell my affairs to any and every saddle tramp? But I will tell you, Sarran. I've been thinking of buying that place. Today seemed like a good time to look it over."

"At sundown?" Pete asked. "And with all your money gone, what would you have used to buy it? Make it a better story than that, Cavendish."

"There's no need to stretch the truth."

Pete smiled thinly and, looking at Avery, asked: "Anything else to tell us?"

The ferryman shook his head, sighing, "No, that's all.

Wish I could be of more help."

"You can," Pete told him. "You know Jeffers, teller in the new bank. Go see if you can find him. Maybe he'll recognize this money. And on your way back you might find Cavendish's saddle and have a look in the pouches for the rest of the money. You might even try his hotel room. Look under the mattress, anywhere. . . ."

"You'll damn' well not!" Cavendish flared, swinging around on Avery. "Anyone who goes through my possibles will have to answer personally to me!"

"Now will they?" Pete asked with a deceptive gentleness.

The Anvil man swung angrily around. Pete lifted the Colt. "Sit down," he ordered. He waited until Cavendish had grudgingly looked around the room and, finding no chair, stepped over to sit on the desk corner. Then Pete nodded to Avery.

"Go ahead," he said.

The slam of the door as the oldster went out seemed to clamp the lid on a weighty silence. That lasted for perhaps half a minute until Brazos, stretching lazily and then rising to stand almost in front of Pete, said belligerently: "Someone's going to pay for this and that someone's not going to be. . . ."

His words broke off. Suddenly Cavendish had moved. The Anvil man, partly obscured from Pete's line of vision, all at once reached back and snatched up the sheriff's Colt. Now he lunged to his feet, leveling the weapon at Pete.

As quickly as thought, catching that hint of movement beyond the outlaw, Pete lunged in behind the man as Cavendish's weapon blasted the silence. Brazos staggered backward and fell into Pete, already collapsing heavily.

The upswinging arc of Pete's .45 was a blur. He had to hesitate a split second until Bob Saunders wheeled out from behind Cavendish, and George Soule dove from his chair for the corner behind the desk. Then Pete squeezed the trigger, feeling the hard pound of the weapon against his wrist at the precise moment that Cavendish's Colt stabbed its red flame at him a second time.

He felt a light touch on his right upper arm. Then he was thumbing another shot, not noticing the abrupt looseness that had come to Cavendish's solid length until it was too late to save his powder. His second bullet straightened the Anvil man as he was falling, so that, when he finally went down, it was sideways onto the desk and then, his knees buckling, to the floor in an awkward sprawl.

After they had carried Cavendish and Brazos over to the back room of the drug store and summoned the coroner, George Soule found three more packets of banknotes in the water pitcher on the bureau in Phil Cavendish's hotel room. A little while later Len Avery walked up to the doctor's with Pete to have the bullet graze on Pete's arm bandaged.

They were well beyond the stores when Avery said: "Well, just let 'em try to get a jury that'll convict Bob and Sam now."

Pete nodded. "Not much chance, is there?" He looked obliquely down at the old ferryman then, adding: "No one ever told me you were such an out-and-out liar, Avery. But thanks for bein' one."

"Who says I'm a liar?" the oldster asked indignantly.

"I do. I want to see the day you'd ride twenty miles to save Phil Cavendish being put out by anything like that rig of yours not working."

Avery's belligerence faded quickly. Then he gave a hearty chuckle. "So do I," he admitted frankly.

Cutbank Welcome

Jon Glidden completed this story near the end of May in 1939 and mailed it off to his agent, Marguerite E. Harper. Probably due to the state of the inventory of stories at Newsstand's Red Circle pulp magazines, the story wasn't purchased until July, 1940. The author was paid the top price at Red Circle: 1½¢ a word. It appeared under the author's title, "Cutbank Welcome for Wet-Cattle Thieves," in *Best Western* (11/40). For its first book appearance this title has been abbreviated.

I

The angry voice of the crowd died as the noose was flicked over the prisoner's neck. The rope was drawn tight. Fifty yards from the cottonwood, lying belly down and peering out through the barn loft door and into the eerie light cast by the flickering pitchpine flares, Jim Walker laid his cheek against the stock of a Winchester and tried to notch the weapon's front sight on the swaying line of the rope.

He was taking a long chance with his own life, a long one with Red Sterling's. The mob was out for blood. Nothing would stop them. Jim knew that his bullet, slanting obliquely down on the impossible chance of severing the rope, might bring down one of the mob. But no man in that crowd was any less guilty of the crime for which Red Sterling was being hanged than Red himself. This thought cooled Jim's nervousness and steadied his hand.

His finger was tightening on the trigger when a voice shouted from the dense shadows out by the street: "You men over there! We've got scatter-guns lined at you! Throw up your hands and step away from Sterling's horse!"

As the crowd hesitated, a few drawing away from the bay pony Red Sterling was roped onto, someone shouted an answer: "Who's 'we', Shaw?"

Jim Walker was faintly surprised at learning that John Hardy, president of the bank, had had the guts to try and stop the job. Then he heard Hardy call again from the street, more menacingly this time: "Me and the sheriff! We'll give you three more seconds to take that rope off Sterling!"

"Like hell . . . ! Put out your torches, men!"

Jim saw the speaker drop his torch and make a dash for

Red Sterling's bay horse. He hit the pony across the rump. The animal shied, and Red Sterling's body was drawn sideways by the tightening rope.

By the light of the last torch, Jim aimed and fired. The brittle *crack* of his rifle marked the sudden snapping of the rope. He saw Red Sterling bend low in the saddle, the broken rope dangling from his neck. The next instant Jim shot again. His bullet burned the pony's flank and the animal lunged clear of the crowd, stretching out to a dead run. There were a few startled shouts, and a gun blazed defiantly into the night while someone called: "Light! We need light!"

Jim didn't wait for more. He ran to the back of the loft, went out its rear opening, and down onto the roof of a lean-to. He jumped from its low roof into the saddle of his roan, bending over to jerk his reins free, and then ram home his spurs.

Four minutes later, far out across the pasture, he picked up a moving shadow ahead and called: "Red?"

Red Sterling's answer carried above the drum of his pony's hoofs: "That you, Jim? God, that was some fancy shootin'!"

Jim rode alongside, caught the bay's trailing reins, and pulled both animals to a quick stop. He jerked the loosened rope from Red's neck, and his clasp knife slashed at the ropes around Red's arms and shoulders as he asked tersely: "You all right?"

Red had caught his breath sharply a moment ago. But now his ruddy face grinned across and he said: "They nicked me. But I ain't dead . . . not by a long ways. Why do you figure Shaw made that play to stop 'em?"

"What Shaw did doesn't matter a damn now," Jim said insistently, for across the pasture he could catch the renewed shouting of the crowd and the sound of at least two horses on the run. There were lights over there, too. "Can you make that Streeter line shack up in the hills?"

"Easy," Red replied, and again Jim detected a catch in his friend's labored breathing. "But where you goin'?"

"I'll toll this mob off your trail. Here's a gun"—Jim handed across one of his twin belts and holsters—"hide your sign, Red, and wait for me at the shack. Tomorrow I'll hop the train at the pass and have a talk with your sister."

Red's face sobered in the shadows. He said gravely: "Don't let Nan get mixed up in a thing like this, Jim. Tell her for me she's to go home again."

"You let me worry about that." Jim slashed the bay with his reins. As Red's horse loped out of sight, he turned the roan at right angles from his friend's trail and set out at a hard run.

With the graying light of dawn outlining the peaks to the east, Jim Walker was waiting along a railroad's right-of-way embankment high in the foothills, listening to the rhythmic pound of a locomotive's exhaust far below him laboring upward toward Mile High Pass. In the past six hours, he had led the posse far astray, covered his sign, and ridden the roan to the top of the pass, now a good five miles away. He'd come these five downward miles afoot, walking the rails as they curved their steep grade around the shoulder of the mountain.

He was wondering now if this errand would net him anything. Red's letter to his sister had been mailed six days ago. She might be on the train or might have waited to take a later one. That was the chance he was running. But whatever train she came in on, he was going to see her before anyone else did.

As the train crawled slowly around the near bend, Jim's tall figure moved into plain sight at the top of the embankment. Two sharp blasts of the whistle let Jim know he'd been seen. He lifted his arm and waved. The engineer returned his salute as the locomotive crawled past, the drive wheels slipping. He swung aboard the combination baggage car-smoker, the only passenger coach, directly behind the tender. As he stepped in off the platform, the conductor left the end seat where he'd been looking in on a poker game played by a whiskey drummer, a 'puncher, and the express clerk, and walked along the swaying aisle back toward him.

Jim handed the conductor two silver dollars, smiling as he drawled: "Me and my jughead parted company down one of them cañons. Give me a ticket to Gody."

The conductor grinned broadly: "Some nags have a bad habit of throwin' a man." He took the money, gave Jim his ticket and change, and went back to the poker game.

Jim turned, touched the brim of his Stetson in a polite gesture of greeting, and said to the girl sitting on the seat nearest the door: "You're Nan Sterling, aren't you?"

She was hatless, tawny-haired, and her face bore a flawless, even beautiful, likeness to Red Sterling's handsome one. Her blue eyes were heavy with sleep and showed only a faint curiosity until Jim spoke. Now they opened wide in surprise and gave her a glowing look of freshness. She said hesitantly: "Yes . . . yes, I'm Nan Sterling."

Jim sat down across from her, and her surprise showed a trace of alarm. He said quietly: "Red sent me. I'm Jim Walker."

"Oh." It was her single statement of understanding, and at the same time she withdrew into a shell of aloofness. "I might have expected something like this."

Jim's lean weather-burned face took on a grave look. "Red's in trouble," he said.

"Has he ever been out of trouble?" There was scorn in her biting rejoinder.

Jim shook his head. "Not many times. But this time it's serious. Last night he came awful close to bein' strung up to a tree. He's up in the hills now, a posse after him, wanted for murder!"

The cloak of indifference fell from Nan Sterling in an instant. She straightened in the seat, breathed—"Murder?"— and was too helpless to go on.

Jim said: "You'll have to listen hard. There isn't much time to talk. I'm leavin' the train at the top of the pass. It. . . ."

"Then you're in trouble, too?" she interrupted him.

"Some. They'll put a reward out for me because of what happened last night. But that doesn't matter. What does . . . is your being here. You'll have to turn around and go back. At least Red says for you to."

"Go back." For a moment there was a helpless, uncertain look in her eyes. Then she added quietly: "I can't go back. I had only money enough to get here."

Jim's anger flared alive. All that had happened these last few days, the fact that Red had written his sister for help, galled him now. He said dryly: "Then you didn't bring him money? Why did you come?" When she merely shrugged and didn't answer, he went on in sarcasm: "Of course, it ain't enough that he's lost his outfit, been framed for murder, and made an outlaw! You've got to come along and be somethin' else to worry about!"

There was sincere humility in her voice as she said gently: "I'm sorry, Jim Walker. I'm only here because I thought I could help." She saved him the embarrassment of having to apologize for his rudeness by saying: "You say Red was framed, that he's lost the place?" She looked stunned, bewildered.

Jim nodded.

"How did it happen?"

"Gamblin'."

She said—"I should have known."—in a lifeless voice.

"Not the kind of gamblin' you're thinkin' of," he told her. "Red's wild and foolish in some ways, but I reckon I'd have done the same. It began last year, right after I came to work for him. You remember that his father left him a mortgage on the place?"

She smiled. "Yes. Father and Red were a lot alike, weren't they?"

"So I hear. Well, Red had this mortgage and was keepin' up the interest and his payments. He didn't gamble much then. Oh, him and me would go in to the Humming Bird now and then and maybe win or lose ten dollars, but it wasn't anything serious with Red. Then he started losin' cattle, not a critter here and there but big bunches of two or three dozen, enough to cripple him. We worked our guts out tryin' to stop it, but it kept on. Last month Red couldn't make the payment on his note. Meantime, he'd lost his hold on himself and was going to the Humming Bird alone, buyin' into those high stake games. The first thing I knew he owed Ed Withers a couple of thousand. And he couldn't pay John Hardy and the bank."

"Then this Ed Withers framed him?" Nan asked.

Jim shook his head, said dryly: "Not exactly. You see, Red was arrested for killin' Withers, for shootin' him in the back."

"Red would never shoot a man in the back! Or anywhere else, unless he had to!"

"You and I know that. The others don't. Withers was honest, even if he did run a saloon. That lynch mob last night thought enough of him to try and string up the man who killed him."

"But you say Red didn't kill him."

"I know he didn't. I was there . . . or practically there . . . when it happened."

"Then why didn't you prove Red didn't do it?"

Jim let out a gusty sigh and explained patiently: "It ain't as easy as it sounds. I'll begin at the beginnin'. First, John Hardy called Red's note. He had a right to do that, seein' that Red was bein' rustled blind and couldn't make good on his note. Instead of lettin' Hardy foreclose and take the outfit, Red went to Ed Withers. Him and me together, late one night after the Humming Bird was closed. Red put it to Withers straight, asking Withers to take over the bank's note. That was to Withers's advantage, since Red owed him money anyway and he'd never stand a prayer of gettin' it back unless he played along with Red. So Withers agreed to it, providin' Red laid off the gamblin'. Red promised."

"And Withers was killed last night?"

Jim nodded. "Right after I left, while they were drawin' up the papers. I'd gone down to the feed barn after the horses. I heard the shot. By the time I got back there, the sheriff was in the office. Withers had a bullet in his spine and Red was lyin' on the floor with a bloody scalp and a smokin' gun in his hand. The sheriff locked Red up. I argued half the night tellin' him what had happened. But the papers were gone. I didn't have any proof."

Nan was silent a long moment, her face gone pale. She said finally: "Wasn't there anyone else to back your story?"

"One man. Tom Dolan. He was swamper for the Humming Bird. He was there that night, cleanin' up the place, and should have heard what went on in the office. He was there when I left, takin' off his apron, gettin' ready to leave. But when the sheriff talked to him, he said he'd gone down the alley and hadn't heard anything. He's a little deaf."

As he talked, a frown changed Nan Sterling's expression and a puzzled look came to her eyes. "Tom Dolan," she murmured. "Haven't I heard that name before?"

"More than likely. Tom used to work with your father."

"Of course!" she said, her look brightening. "He was helping Dad dig that test hole up along the north fence. That test hole," she stated, coloring slightly, "was the reason Mother left my father."

Jim nodded. He'd heard the story of old Bob Sterling's separation from his wife. A desert-bitten prospector, Bob Sterling had never taken very seriously the business of ranching. Even after promising to forget prospecting when he was married, he'd put every extra dollar of his money into the test hole he and Tom Dolan had put down up along the north fence of the ranch. Nan's mother, in the end miserable to see her family deprived of necessities because of her husband's fruitless attempts at finding gold, took her daughter and left the ranch. Red had stayed with his father who, too late, realized his mistake. True to a stern code, Bob Sterling had dynamited the test hole and never worked it after his wife's leaving. He died a lonely old man, striving as well as he knew how to make good his mistake by putting all his efforts toward saving the ranch. He hadn't quite managed it and had left Red a mortgage.

Now Nan said: "Tom Dolan and Father never got on well. I heard that they had quite a fight right after mother left."

"Dolan didn't approve of blowin' up two years of hard work with giant powder," Jim said. "No prospector alive likes to see a thing like that. It gets in their blood."

"And he couldn't help you prove Red was innocent?"

Jim shrugged his shoulders. "Either couldn't or wouldn't. He doesn't think much of anyone by the name of Sterling." He looked out the window at the slow-moving pattern of the nearest piñon-studded slope. "I've got to be leavin'."

As he got up from the seat, Nan said hastily: "But . . . but what am I to do?"

"Go back to Kansas City."

"I told you I can't. I don't have the money."

Bleakly Jim considered this. In the end, he said: "I'll write you a note to the bank. I've got a hundred dollars I won't be needin'."

Nan shook her head, smiling up at him. "No, Jim. I couldn't accept it. I . . . I think I'll stay. Maybe I can help."

"You can't stay. They'll make it hard for you."

"This banker," she said, ignoring what he had told her. "What was his name?"

"John Hardy."

"Couldn't I go to see him?"

"You could. But it wouldn't help much."

"He might give me . . . give Red . . . another chance."

Jim moved his head in a slow negative. "It's up to you. If you're stayin' and want to see Hardy, there's something else you might do. It's been pretty hot for me down there in town. I've been meanin' to have a talk with Tom Dolan but haven't had the chance. I just might be able to get something out of Dolan. Now that Red's safe for a few days, I'd like to try seein' him again."

"Couldn't I talk to him?"

"No. But I could. Here's what you do. Today, after you see Hardy, find out if Tom Dolan's around town, find out where he's stayin'. Tonight I'll meet you by that lean-to behind the old barn at the west end of the street. You can tell me where Dolan is then. I'll be there about nine. Don't let anyone follow you out to the barn."

An obvious alarm was in Nan's eyes now. "Can you do that, Jim . . . without running too big a chance?" Then, before he had the chance to reply, she went on: "Why are you doing this for Red, for me? Why not let Red do it?"

"Red's got to hide out," he told her. "Besides, Red pays me wages. I reckon it won't hurt to earn 'em."

"Not wages to fight for him, though."

"No, not fightin' wages. But there's something else. I figure Red got a raw deal. I aim to find out who framed him . . . just so him and me will be able to hold up our heads around here."

As he reached out to open the door, Nan was about to say something. Before she could, the 'puncher sitting in the poker game at the front end of the car stepped into the aisle and called: "Hold on! Ain't you Jim Walker?"

Jim's right hand came down from the knob of the door to hang within finger spread of his holster. He said: "That's my handle. Why?"

The 'puncher was uncertain now. He gave the conductor a glance, said: "What did that wire say about that Red Sterling gettin' away last night, Bill?"

The conductor's hand was traveling to a pocket of his coat when Jim's hand rose smoothly along his thigh to rock a .45 Colt into line with the group at the far end of the car. He drawled: "I'll save you the trouble of lookin'! Red Sterling got away from a lynch mob last night. I was the one who got him away." The 'puncher's face turned a sickly yellow at sight of the gun. He swore acidly, and Jim, with a glance out the window, added—"I'll be hightailin', gents!"—and opened the door. He gave Nan a last quick look, tempered by a smile, and, as he swung down off the platform to run three strides along the embankment, he had the picture of her oval face firmly engraved on his mind. His roan was standing in the coulée less than two hundred yards below the spot he had left the train.

★ ★ ★ ★ ★

Late that afternoon he reined in at the edge of a clearing high in the aspen country that footed the peaks. For three long minutes he sat with a rifle cradled across his arm, studying a small slab shack at the clearing's center. Red Sterling's bay pony grazed a few feet out from the shack. The bay was saddled and the reins were trailing, two facts that worried Jim. Other things that put the deep frown on his face were the absence of any smoke coming from the squat stone chimney and the wide open door.

He came down out of the saddle, worked around through the trees at the back of the shack, and only then approached it quickly. He hugged the wall as he worked around to the side. He took off his Stetson and edged over until he was staring in through the small dusty window.

What he saw brought him wheeling quickly around to the front and in the door. He stopped two strides inside the door, staring blankly at the cabin's single bunk. Red Sterling laid there, face up, eyes open and fixed vacantly on the sloping timbers of the roof. The dirty blanket he lay on was stained darkly with a smear that led to a glistening wet puddle of blood on the floor. Red Sterling was dead.

II

Riding into the far end of the town's street that night, past the barn a good hour before the time he'd agreed to meet Nan Sterling, Jim Walker's thoughts were dark and brooding under the heavy blanket of a deep-rooted bitterness. Red Sterling had died from the bullet of the gun that exploded so wildly last night under the cottonwood that was to have served the mob as a gallows. Red, wild, reckless, unstable, hadn't deserved to die. The unfairness of the thing galled Jim more than anything that had ever happened to him.

He was weary to the bone, hungry and beaten. But, he told himself, now was no time to give up. Perhaps the memory of Nan Sterling, of those few minutes he had known her, was what served to make him go on, to swear solemnly to himself that he would untangle this maze of trickery that had started with Ed Withers's death. His arms and hands ached from the labor it had taken him to gouge out a shallow grave for Red, a grave he'd piled high with stones in that lonely clearing in the hills. On the way down out of the hills he'd killed a cottontail and grilled it over a glowing bed of cedar coals. Later he'd stripped and bathed in a cold mountain stream. That slim meal and the shock of the cold water had braced him to the task he now faced.

He was going to see John Hardy, to plead with the banker to give Nan Sterling a chance to come into her rightful inheritance. The ranch wasn't much, but it could be made to pay in the end. It would be a far better life for Nan than the dreary and friendless job she'd had since her mother's death, teaching in a small country school back on the desolate Kansas prairie. Jim had already decided that he'd help Nan work the ranch, put the place back on its feet, and lift it clear of the mortgage. That was the best he could do for Red's memory.

He knew the Hardy place, a big white frame house far out toward this end of the street. Hardy was a bachelor and used a housekeeper, a woman who didn't live in the place. The street was dark, shaded from the starlight by a towering arch of cottonwoods.

Jim boldly turned in at the hitching post beyond the walk. He tied the roan and went in through the gate of the picket fence and up onto the porch. He knocked on the door and heard a man's slow step cross the hallway beyond.

It was John Hardy who opened the door, his thin dark face going immediately slack in surprise when he saw who it was. He was a tall man, nearly as tall as Jim, and thin and severe-looking in a suit of black broadcloth and a white shirt. He wore spectacles and now reached up to take them off in a deliberate gesture that was typical of him.

Jim said: "Busy, Hardy?"

"No. Come in." There was no surprise on the banker's face. It was as though Jim were an ordinary caller that he had been expecting. Jim entered, stepping to one side of the door. Hardy smiled thinly as he caught the meaning behind the move. He said: "Careful, aren't you?"

Jim nodded, and Hardy closed the door and led the way into a room off the right of the hallway. It was a small living room, with a lamp burning dimly on the table at its center. Hardy went to the broad bay window that faced the street and pulled down the shades before he turned up the lamp. Then, motioning to a chair, he said: "Sit down?"

"What I came to say can be said standin'," Jim assured him.

"And what's that?"

"You've seen the girl, Red's sister?"

Hardy nodded. "Very attractive."

"What sort of a deal did you make with her?"

"Deal?" Hardy feigned misunderstanding. "What sort of a deal could I make?"

"Then you're takin' over the lay-out?"

"Much as I dislike it, yes. Since seeing Miss Sterling, I regret having to do it. She's half owner, I believe."

"The place is worth more than the amount of the note."

Hardy shrugged his bony shoulders. "That's unfortunate and I realize it. I'll call an auction, of course." Slowly his look hardened. "But, remember, it's Red Sterling and not his sister I'm dealing with! I have hopes that there won't be a dollar left once the auction's over. In fact, I'm counting on buying it myself, at the face value of the note."

"Supposin' I tell you Red's dead."

Hardy's surprise was genuine but brief. He smiled, a thin smile with no warmth in it. "What's your play, Walker?"

"That's on the level. Red died last night in a shack up in the hills above Streeter's place. Go up there and you'll find the grave."

There was a moment's silence, in which Hardy took a white handkerchief from his pocket and began polishing his spectacles. He shrugged. "Should I be sorry?"

"I don't expect you to. The other night you wouldn't believe he was innocent of that murder and you don't believe it yet. But this sister of his . . . she's broke, here without even enough to buy her train fare back to Kansas City."

"Perhaps I can arrange to buy a ticket for her."

"That's all? You won't give her another chance? I'll help her get the place on its feet again."

Hardy shook his head. "Why should I? She means nothing to me. Besides, it would be poor business."

Jim cursed soundly, his anger flaring. "You're stealin' it, Hardy!"

"Possibly," the banker said smugly. "But you're a poor man to be telling me what to do. The last I heard there was a reward on your head."

"Want to try collectin' it?" Jim asked, unsurprised at hearing of something he had known would happen.

"And no one invited you to come here," Hardy went on, ignoring the jibe. He finished polishing his glasses, and his hand returned to his hip pocket as he added: "I long ago formed a habit of providing for unwelcome guests, Walker. A little matter of dropping a certain object in this pocket before I answer the door at night."

His hand came smoothly around from his pocket. He was fisting a pearl-handled Derringer that looked ridiculously small in his long-fingered hand. The move was so unexpected, his words had been so even toned, that Jim was caught with hands at his sides, taken completely by surprise.

Hardy went on in that same monotonous drawl: "Raise your hands, Walker. I'm coming over to get your gun. I'll warn you that this is loaded with buckshot."

He stepped in close to Jim and lifted his gun from the holster. Then, out of reach again, he laid Jim's gun on the center table and motioned to the door. "If you'll step out there, I'll telephone the sheriff to come get you." He circled Jim and backed through the doorway, a broad one with a panel that slid back into the partition. "Stand here where I can see you, Walker."

Jim came into the doorway, hands at the level of his shoulders, and leaned against the frame. The panel slid an inch or two back into the partition under his weight. Across the hallway, Hardy stood sideways, Derringer in his right hand and his left going up to lift the receiver from its prongs on the wall telephone. Only then did the banker seem to remember that he had to ring to call the operator. He reached up with his gun hand to hold down the receiver cradle, turning the bell knob with the other, his eyes on Jim across the hallway.

Jim's upraised left hand touched the door and he looked up lazily and appeared to be studying a molding on the ornately plastered ceiling. But suddenly his body lunged sideward, across the spread of the doorway. His left hand, closing on the door, pulled it out of the wall as he wheeled back inside the room.

John Hardy moved a split second after Jim. He dropped the receiver and his hand whipped down, throwing the Derringer into line. He saw the edge of Jim's shirt vanish behind the closing door panel and shot squarely through the quarter inch planking. The explosion made the front windows of the hallway rattle with the concussion. A jagged six inch hole showed in the panel. The hole was waist high, mute evidence of the Derringer's killing power at close range.

A satisfied smile crossed the banker's face. He broke open the breech of the Derringer, took out the twelve-gauge brass shell case, and blew the smoke from the barrel. Then, laying it on the hallway table, he crossed to throw open the door again, his glance first traveling to the floor immediately behind the door, where he knew Jim Walker would be lying dead.

"Good thing I ducked in behind the wall, wasn't it?" came Jim's quiet voice. He stood spraddle-legged, beyond the center table. His gun was in the holster, seeming to make a mockery of Hardy's confidence. "Any more of those toys tucked in your pockets, Hardy?"

The banker's face lost color but its expression was impassive, neither angry nor hateful. "No," he said.

"I'll be leavin', the way I came." Jim came across the

room, stepped past Hardy, and went out into the hallway. He glanced toward the phone—"Just in case you get any fancy notions, Hardy."—and took a hold on the long neck of the mouthpiece and wrenched the instrument and its box from the wall.

Outside, he went unhurriedly down the walk. As he reined the roan out into the street, he heard the front door of an adjoining house slam. He rode out the street as the neighbor, curious over the shot, ran up John Hardy's front walk and knocked loudly on the door.

Nan was waiting by the lean-to behind the barn. She came out of the shadows as Jim walked his horse in toward the shed. She called softly, urgently: "Jim, you were in town!"

He motioned her to silence and came down out of the saddle as the hoof clatter of running horses echoed out along the street. In ten more seconds a knot of six riders boiled past, heading into open country, less than fifty yards out from the place Jim and Nan stood.

"After you?" Nan asked.

Jim nodded and told her of his visit to John Hardy.

Her look was grave when he had finished. "You shouldn't be taking these chances for me and Red," she murmured. "Hardy might have killed you."

"I'm fair game," he told her. "But Red isn't . . . not any more."

Her look swung up on him and with some strange intuitive insight she breathed: "Red's dead!"

"Yes." He waited, loathing himself for his abruptness.

She looked away and for a long moment was silent. He saw her hand come up. It held a filmy white handkerchief. Then she was facing him again, smiling bravely, saying: "Nothing we can do will bring him back, will it, Jim? You did all you could. Now you can ride away from all this."

He said quietly—"No."—and waited as she caught the full implication of his single word before he added: "I won't let it end like this. For you, for me, and for Red. Someone killed Ed Withers. I intend to find out who that someone was."

"But Jim, it's so . . . so. . . ."

"It's my job. I'd never be able to live with my conscience if I didn't try. Hardy won't give in. We've got one more thing. Tom Dolan."

"And he's gone," Nan said. "The saloon's closed, and Dolan left yesterday. While I was asking the clerk in the hotel about him, a man came up who'd seen him in Timberline yesterday. Is Timberline a town?"

"Stage station. What was Dolan doing up there?"

"The man didn't know. But he said Dolan was drunk and losing a lot of money in a game of poker that had been going on since the night before. He. . . ."

Suddenly Jim reached out and took Nan by the arm in a grip that made her wince. "Say that again," he breathed. "Dolan drunk and losin' money in a poker game?"

She nodded, moving her arms a little and laughing nervously as she said: "Jim, you're hurting me."

"Sorry." His hold relaxed. "But this is important. Tom Dolan was flat broke a week ago. I know because he borrowed five dollars from me to last him until next pay day. Where would he get the money to go on a bat and keep him in a poker session a night and a day? They play a stiff game up there at Timberline."

"I don't know, Jim. Where would he?"

"He didn't steal it or it would be all over town."

"Then?"

"And why would he leave town? He's lived here for thirty years, accordin' to Red. He couldn't earn a livin'

70

anywhere else. Ed Withers gave him that swampin' job just to keep him off the street."

All at once Nan said, low-voiced: "Someone gave him the money?"

"Looks like it." Jim took tobacco and papers from his shirt pocket and built a smoke. Nan noticed that his hands weren't very steady.

"Jim, is this . . . does this mean that Dolan can help us?" She had made a wild guess, the only one that gave a ready explanation for Jim's nervousness.

"I won't lay any bets on it." He threw the cigarette away, as he remembered that someone might be watching and see the flare of his match. He went on intently: "Get back to the hotel, Nan. Stay away from John Hardy. Now that he knows Red's dead, he may try to wind this thing up quick. Don't sign anything! I'll see you here tomorrow night."

He turned and had taken a step toward his horse when she said—"Jim."—in a tone that stopped him. She came over to him. "What are you going to do?"

"Find out where Dolan got that money, and why."

"Will it be . . . dangerous?"

He laughed. "Dolan never carries a gun."

"But those other men he's with at Timberline."

His look hardened. "They won't know me."

"Be careful, Jim," she said softly. And, as he turned away again, added: "I'll be waiting for you."

III

Jim had no illusions riding up to Ted Snow's Timberline stage station. For years Snow had carefully maintained his contract with the stage line, supplying four fresh and well-fed teams each day for the east and west runs, only so that he could conduct his real business, the running of a small bar and gambling lay-out. Here, in an isolated spot high along the pass trail, a professional gambler could drop his luggage off the stage and spend as long or as short a time as he wanted matching his skill with outlaws, saddle tramps, and the night-riding outcasts from the gambling lay-outs of the valley towns below. These last were many, for the law in this country made it hard for a man caught cheating at cards. Jim knew, as he swung out of the saddle below the dimly lit window of Timberline's squat stone headquarters, that none of Snow's regular customers would pass up the chance of collecting the reward on him if he were recognized.

He had ridden a rangy black gelding the twelve miles up here. The roan, worn down from two days of hard saddle work, was in the pasture of the black's owner back in the valley. Jim intended returning the black and changing again to the roan, once his own horse had rested a day or two. With luck, the rancher who owned the black wouldn't discover the exchange.

As he climbed the stone steps toward the door of Ted Snow's bar, Jim reached down to ease his gun in its holster. He had made no plan beyond deciding that he wouldn't leave here without Tom Dolan, or without having talked to him. As he opened the door, he breathed a rush of warm stale air, smoky, foul with the sour smell of beer and whiskey. He

72

swept the small smoke-fogged room with a glance, seeing that Tom Dolan was one of the four players at the table to the right and that Snow was alone at his crude pine bar, perched on a stool and dozing with his head on his arms.

His closing of the door made Snow lift his head and brought the glances of the others around on him, all but Tom Dolan's, whose eyes were fixed in a drunk's vacant stare on the cards held awkwardly fanwise in his hand.

Jim was relieved at seeing that the three men at the table with Dolan were strangers. He said—"Howdy, Ted."—and sauntered over toward Snow, ignoring the others. He wasn't worrying about the stage station owner, for the ethics of Snow's business demanded that he shouldn't betray the presence of a wanted man.

Snow said: " 'Mornin', Jim. Have a drink?" He reached for a bottle of bourbon as Jim leaned on the bar. Then, uncorking the bottle, he added in a tone too low for the others to hear: "Tom's bein' taken for a cleanin'. Too drunk to see the spots on the pasteboards. You better leave before the same happens to you."

There was a faint look of alarm on Snow's face that Jim didn't understand. Jim said: "I don't get it, Ted."

Snow nodded toward the door. "Two deputies dropped in less'n ten minutes ago. They're lookin' for you."

"Oh, that." Jim laughed softly and drained his shot glass of whiskey.

"I mean it, Jim. You'd better hightail. They claimed they're coverin' all the trails, sure of gettin' you this time. It seems that John Hardy didn't much like the call you paid him."

"I came up here for Tom," Jim stated.

Snow's narrow-slitted eyes opened wider. He smiled mirthlessly. "Try and break into that game! I have. Those jaspers have seen his roll. He's theirs until he loses his last greenback!"

"You goin' to make a kick if I try, Ted?"

The station owner hesitated, then said flatly: "Hell, no! They've been here two nights straight runnin' and I could stand some sleep. Only you pay for any damage, Jim. You ain't wreckin' the place." He paused long enough to let his words carry their weight, then asked: "How's Red?"

"So-so," Jim told him, pushing out from the bar and going across to stand by the table.

He stood there a full minute, trying to catch Tom Dolan's eye and not succeeding. At the end of that interval the man whose chair he stood behind looked up over his shoulder and drawled dryly: "Move away, stranger!"

Jim had been waiting for something like this. This trio was typical of the hard-faced, shifty-eyed breed that traveled these obscure trails on even more obscure errands. They all wore guns. They were ready for trouble, unlike Tom Dolan who had glanced up at Jim a moment ago and failed to recognize him through the whiskey fog that slowed his brain.

Jim had been long trained in the school these men represented. The only language they understood was one as salty as their own; the only thing they respected, or feared, was a fast hand with a gun and a set of guts to back it. So now he looked down into the unshaven square face of the man who had spoken. "I like it here!" He hooked his thumbs in his belt and waited.

The man's unwinking stare showed anger. He swore softly, and put his hands on the arms of his chair, as though to rise. But something in Jim's look stopped him. He turned back to the table, glanced significantly at his companions, and growled: "Ben, it's your raise!"

The man to his left threw five blue chips into the pot, ignoring Jim completely. It was Tom Dolan's turn now. Tom rubbed his hand across his eyes, looked at his cards once more, and muttered thickly—"I'm out."—folding his hand.

"The hell you're out!" growled the player whose challenge had failed to move Jim from behind his chair. "You had openers. Bet 'em!"

"Tell him to go to hell, Tom," Jim drawled.

As the man wheeled in the chair to face him again, Jim heard faintly the rattling echoes of two ponies coming down the trail. He forgot that as the man snarled: "Stranger, haul your carcass away from here before we haul it for you!"

Jim challenged—"Start haulin'!"—and threw his boot out in an arc that swept the man's chair from under him.

As he sprawled to the floor, the other pair lunged up out of their chairs, hands stabbing down at holsters. Jim's arm blurred down and up, settling his .45 at the level of his waist. The two men facing him raised their hands as the third picked himself up from the floor and wheeled on Jim, crouched for a lunge. Before he could move, Jim stepped in, feinting a blow with his left. As the man's right hand laced out at him, Jim dodged and brought the barrel of his gun down in a swift sure blow. The man's knees buckled as the gun raked his scalp above his ear. He went down like a half full sack of grain, loosely, awkwardly, stunned.

The other pair hadn't moved. Tom Dolan was still in his chair. But now he stared up at Jim with slow comprehension.

Jim said: "Comin', Tom?"

"Where?" Dolan asked thickly, his face taking on color as a hostile light came into his watery blue eyes.

Jim heard the door hinges grate behind him and half turned to look back over his shoulder. A chunky short man stood in the door, a gun in his hand. He wore a deputy sheriff's badge pinned to his vest.

He called: "Make your play, Walker, or drop that hogleg!" As he spoke, another man came in the door to stand beside him. Jim recognized this last man as the owner of the gelding he had traded for the roan tonight. Jim's gun was out of line with the deputy. He'd be dropped before he could get in a shot. He let go his gun and raised his hands as it thudded to the plank floor.

The last man in saw Jim, recognized him, and exploded: "By God, it's Walker! It's him that rode the black of mine up here!" He whistled softly. "Ain't every day a man can collect a reward by runnin' onto a stolen horse. We split that money even between us, don't we, Mills?"

The deputy nodded, saying: "And stealin' a horse is a hangin' offense, Walker."

Jim's let-down over his failure brought on the bitter thought that he had lost his grip on the last slender thread that might help him untangle the web of circumstance surrounding Red Sterling's frame-up. In another thirty seconds he'd have had Tom Dolan out of here, had his chance to get the oldster's story of where he got his money. Now that chance was gone and Nan, alone, would never find the answer.

The deputy was staring beyond Jim, sizing up the men at the table. He saw Tom Dolan and said dryly: "Haven't they cleaned you yet, Tom?" He had evidently heard the story Nan had heard tonight.

Dolan replied stubbornly: "Whose business is it what I do with my money?"

Jim had a sudden inspired thought that made him say: "It's my business, Tom!"

Every eye in the room swung on Jim. He turned and looked at Ted Snow, who still sat on the stool behind the bar. The look on Snow's face was one of wariness. Jim asked:

"Ted, Dolan came up here Thursday night, didn't he?"

Snow nodded cautiously.

"And he had three hundred dollars in that roll, didn't he?" Jim was making a wild guess.

The station owner shrugged his shoulders. "How should I know how much he had?"

Jim turned to the table, to the men who had been in the game with Dolan. "Didn't he?" he asked them.

Tom Dolan flared. "It was five hundred, even! And what the hell is it to you?"

"It was three hundred dollars, Tom. The three hundred Red paid Withers that night Withers was killed. The night you were swampin' out the joint when I left. You were there when the shot was fired. You ran into the office, saw both men on the floor, and saw the money. You took the money and hightailed before the sheriff barged in!" He nodded to the deputy. "If you won't take him on your own, I'll swear out a warrant for Dolan's arrest! You can hold him until you check my story, Mills."

Tom Dolan lunged drunkenly out from the table, cursing in his rage at Jim's trumped-up story. He struck out at Jim, and Jim hit him a light blow across the face that spun him around and dropped him to his knees.

The deputy said sharply—"Hold a gun on Walker, Bates!"—and came across the room to flick a pair of handcuffs around Tom Dolan's wrists. "Take it easy, Tom," he advised. "Walker's story sounds fishy as hell to me. But I've got to hold you until we can check on it." He looked up at Jim. "Why wasn't that money mentioned the other night when you had your talk with the sheriff?"

Jim added another lie: "I saw the money was missin' and thought, if I could find the man who took it, I'd know who killed Withers. Red didn't."

"Yeah?" jibed the deputy, helping Dolan to his feet. He eyed the trio who had been in the game with the oldster, saying curtly: "You jaspers hit the trail out! Be across the country line by sunup or I'll have warrants out for you!"

The man Jim had gun-whipped came uncertainly to his feet. He and the other two moved sullenly across to the door, one of them calling back before he went out: "Dolan's right. He had more than three hundred in that roll."

"Beat it!" the deputy told him. "We'll decide whether Dolan's guilty or not." When they had gone, he nodded to Jim. "Get goin', Walker. I'd hate like hell to be standin' in your boots right now!"

IV

John Hardy was one of the few men on hand to witness the arrival of the deputy and his prisoners. He didn't approve of Tom Dolan's being jailed but seemed satisfied when he heard why he had been brought in, commenting dryly: "Walker made up that cock and bull story. If Red Sterling had had any money, he'd have paid it toward his note. But go ahead, Mills. Dolan can sober up in here just as well as any place else. He'll be out by morning."

After Mills had locked up the jail and cleared the office out front of the crowd, things quieted down. Tom Dolan's whistling snore was the only thing that broke the silence, the only thing that saved Jim from giving away to the futility of all he'd done in these long hours since he had ridden in on the hill shack to find Red Sterling dead. Those snores represented to Jim his last and only hope, and that a small one.

The jail was of adobe three feet thick, dirt-floored, and with only two openings, the steel door at the end of the corridor and a barred open window high up in the wall of Tom Dolan's cell, the adjoining one. Had the window been in Jim's cell, he might have tried to think of a way out. As it was, there was no way of escaping. The gratings at the ends of the cells were of tooled steel and the locks were strong. If he'd had several days, a week maybe, he'd have found some way of breaking out. As it was, he knew that to stay in here longer than twenty-four hours might see him dead. For all the resentment that had been directed to Red over Withers's death would turn on him now. Tomorrow, perhaps the day after, whoever was behind this would prod a mob into a frenzy that would end in another lynching.

The thing to do was to get Tom Dolan's story. Jim peered through the bars and into the oldster's cell. Dolan lay on his cot along the rear wall. The cot was out of reach.

Jim called softly—"Tom."—and the snores continued. He called louder—"Dolan!"—but still there was no let-up in the heavy breathing from the cot. Nothing would wake the old swamper until morning . . . unless. . . .

Jim went down on to his knees and reached over into Dolan's cell as far as he could. His hand was a foot and a half short of the near end of the cot. He tried wedging his shoulder through the bars and gained another six inches. Then he took off his belt and fashioned a loop in one end of it by using the buckle.

He reached through again, and tossed the loop over the two-inch end of one of the crossed legs that stuck up above the foot of the cot. Slowly, pulling evenly, he moved the cot a foot, two. Then he laid the belt aside and caught hold with his hand and pulled until the cot's foot was against the bars. He reached over and shook one of Dolan's boots, calling again: "Tom!" Still the snores went on.

It took him longer to pull the cot in so that its length lay along the side wall of the cell. But in the end he could reach through and grab Dolan by the hair and shake his head.

He had rocked the oldster's head roughly twice from side to side when a hint of sound came from the window high in the wall of Dolan's cell.

Boom!

An orange flash of light came from the window with a gun's exploding concussion. Jim's ears were still ringing when something thudded to the floor of the cell beyond. An instant later the key grated in the lock of the jail door, the door swung open and Mills, a gun in one hand, a lantern in the other, strode in bellowing: "What the hell's goin' on here?"

Jim said quickly: "Bring that light over!"

"Get your hands up, damn you, Walker!" Mills snarled. Then, when Jim's hands were raised, he stepped to the door of the cell.

By the light of the lantern, Jim could see John Hardy's pearl-handled Derringer lying on the floor alongside a four-inch-deep hole that had been gouged in the dirt. The hole was on a line with the place Tom Dolan's head would have been had his cot remained unmoved.

Jim said quietly: "Looks like someone didn't want Tom ever to wake up."

Mills was dumbfounded, bewildered. While he was groping for an answer to this, having seen the Derringer, the position of Dolan's cot, and the open window above the hole, he said curtly: "Keep your hands lifted, Walker!"

Tom Dolan still snored. Jim nodded toward the door. "Better keep everyone out until I've told you what I know, Mills."

The deputy was uncertain, his gun lined rock steady at Jim.

Jim went on: "I think I've got the answer for you. But close that door! Don't let anyone in."

"Shove your hands through them bars," Mills ordered. "Damned if I take another chance with you."

Jim obeyed, and Mills flicked a pair of handcuffs over his wrists. He had started down the corridor for the door when muffled voices sounded in the office beyond.

Jim said again urgently—"Don't let anyone in, Mills."— and Mills opened the office door a crack to shout: "Quiet in there!"

John Hardy's voice called from the office—"Anything wrong, Mills?"—but Mills closed the door without answering, muttering: "Goddlemighty, I wish the sheriff wasn't out hellin' around the country with that posse!"

Jim said quickly: "Get back here, Mills. Carry Dolan into that other cell! Sit him against the back wall in the corner where the light won't reach him. He won't snore that way, either. Move his cot against the back wall and roll up his blanket so it looks like someone lyin' there. Throw my blanket over it and it'll look like Tom's dead and you've covered his face. Lay the Derringer on the floor close by. Move, man!"

Mills said suspiciously: "Why? Who's givin' orders around here?"

"Damn it!" Jim exploded. "Use your head for once! Ask yourself the same thing I was goin' to ask Dolan after I dragged his cot over here to reach him. Where did Dolan get that roll of money? I was runnin' a sandy when I said it was Red's. Someone paid Dolan to leave town because of what he saw the night Withers was killed. Whoever it was shot through the window just now tryin' to make sure Dolan wouldn't ever talk again. He'd be dead if I hadn't been so anxious to get my hands on him and beat the truth out of him."

"How do I know you ain't runnin' a sandy?" Mills was still unconvinced.

"You don't have to take my word for it. Get things fixed the way I said and ask John Hardy to step in here. That's John Hardy's Derringer."

Mills breathed incredulously—"The hell you say!"—and reached for his keys. He moved Tom Dolan into the jail's rear cell, sitting the oldster in the far corner. Dolan's snores didn't break off, so Jim called —"Stick something in his mouth."— and Mills stuffed his bandanna in between Dolan's teeth and tied it in place. After that, Dolan breathed evenly, so softly that Jim couldn't hear him.

As he arranged the cot and blankets in Dolan's cell, the deputy looked at Jim once. "I can't figure this out. Either I'm havin' a nightmare and you're tellin' the truth or you've got something up your sleeve, Walker. John Hardy? Hell, I can't take it all in."

Jim moved his hands, still handcuffed to the door of his cell. "I can't do you much harm this way, Mills. All I ask you to do is get John Hardy in here and tell him Tom Dolan's dead. Leave the rest to me. You'll have to back what I say."

Mills shrugged. "I ain't got nothin' to lose."

As the deputy started toward the jail door, Jim thought of one more thing. "Tell Hardy I killed Dolan. That's why you've got me handcuffed here."

Mills grinned broadly. "That's one thing I know for sure. You couldn't have done it. I went over you with a fine-toothed comb up at Timberline. All you packed in here was a sack of tobacco, three matches, and sixty-seven cents in small change."

He opened the door and stood in it, listening to the jumble of questions shot at him by the half dozen men in the office who had heard the shot from the street and come to see what had happened. He motioned them to silence, saying solemnly: "Tom Dolan's dead, gents. Walker did it. Hardy, give me a hand in here."

It was better than Jim hoped for. Mills was using his head.

John Hardy stepped down the corridor, followed by Mills who carried the lantern. Mills had locked the office door. The banker muttered—"Tom Dolan dead."—as though he didn't believe it. He stopped in front of the empty cell, looked in at the blanket-draped cot that covered the hole in the floor. Then his glance slowly came around to Jim. His pale gray eyes were surface-glinted, cold.

"You'll hang for this, Walker."

Jim said: "I didn't do it."

Mills flared in mock anger. "Didn't, huh! There's the gun. There's the body."

"Someone shot through the window at Dolan," Jim said. "You can see the window's open."

Mills was stumped for a moment, but presently he said: "Sure, because I opened it when I locked Tom up. I hope to hell I get the chance to pull the trap from under you, Walker."

John Hardy's glance had gone back to Tom Dolan's cot again. He seemed to see the Derringer for the first time. He said quickly: "That's my gun! Now I know Walker did it! Mills, I tried to wing Walker with that Derringer at my house. He got it away from me and took it with him." His hard gaze settled on Jim. "Walker, I'll personally accuse you of murder at your trial . . . if you live to stand trial."

A significant look passed between Mills and Jim. The deputy stepped over to the door of Jim's cell, his back to his prisoner. He set the lantern on the floor, hooked his thumbs in his gun belt, and leaned back against the door. "Hardy, you're a damned liar!"

Hardy's lower jaw thrust out in the set of anger. He said: "Watch your tongue, Mills!"

"I said you're a damned liar!" Mills repeated. "Take a look under the blanket on that cot."

Hardy's look was a little uncertain now. He stepped into Dolan's cell and threw back the blanket. His face was perfectly impassive as he saw the rolled blanket underneath. Mills said: "Move the cot away and look at the floor." Hardy did that, too, seeing all there was to see.

When the banker straightened from his inspection, Mills went on: "I know Walker didn't do it because he couldn't have been up there shootin' down from the window. Another thing. I searched him before I brought him in tonight. I ain't

84

sure how many buttons there is on his underwear, but I'm damned sure he wasn't packin' that belly-gun!"

Hardy said blankly: "Then who did it? Who did you give that gun to, Walker?" He walked back out of the cell again.

Jim, his level gaze fixing the banker, said: "You killed Withers in the Humming Bird, Hardy. You knew we were goin' to see Withers that night. You clubbed Red from behind and put the gun in his hand afterward. Tom Dolan saw or heard enough to make it worth your while to pay him five hundred dollars to leave the country. You should have killed him then instead of waitin' until tonight. That was your mistake. Tomorrow mornin', when he sobers up, the sheriff will get his story."

Hardy was smiling now confidently. "And why did I do all this, Walker? You might as well make a good story of it so long as you've started."

"I'll make it good. Why did you do it? Because you want Red's lay-out."

Hardy laughed aloud. "That ten-cow outfit? Why should I want it when I already own upwards of fifty sections of graze that makes the Sterling place look like a nester's lay-out?"

Jim had no answer for that, and, as he hesitated, Hardy laughed again. "I'll admit your story's convincing, Walker. It might hold water but for a couple of things. First, the Sterling place isn't worth a nickel beyond the amount of the note. Second, you took that Derringer. Who shot through the window and tried to frame me? Red?"

Mills looked around at Jim. There was doubt in the deputy's eyes now. He said: "Well, Walker? How about it?"

"Red's dead," Jim said. "I told you that tonight, Hardy. Get his sister and she'll prove it."

"You could both be lying," Hardy said.

A scraping sound came from the end cell. As Hardy turned

85

to face it, Tom Dolan's choking voice said: "Who stuffed this damn' rag in my mouth?"

They could vaguely see him moving then. He pulled himself to his feet and staggered to the door of the cell, still drunk. He stood there, tottering uncertainly on his heels, looking at John Hardy. He drawled thickly: "I been listenin', John. You want me to tell 'em why you'd like to have the Sterling lay-out?"

"Go back and sleep it off," Hardy said quickly. "You're drunk, Tom."

"Drunk, am I?" Dolan muttered, incensed at the suggestion. "Who the hell says I'm drunk? How about some more *dinero,* Hardy? I've about run through that. . . ."

Jim yelled—"Down, Tom!"—as John Hardy's right hand slashed up under the front of his coat toward his left armpit.

Tom Dolan went down, not because he wanted to but because he'd lost his hold on the cell door and was too drunk to stand unsupported. Hardy's hand arced down and the gun he fisted, a short barreled .38 Colt, exploded once.

Jim moved his feet and hands at the same time. Mills's back was to him. Running his manacled hands down the bars, he snatched the deputy's gun from its holster and lifted his right boot to push Mills out of the way.

As Mills went to his knees under the drive of Jim's boot, Jim said—"Turn around, Hardy!"—his voice sounding on the heel of the banker's shot.

Hardy spun around, his gun coming into line. He shot once, twice, hurrying as he saw the deputy's gun in Jim's hand rising up at him. Jim triggered one shot before his right hand opened under the slam of Hardy's third bullet that took him in the shoulder. His tall frame went rigid in expectation of the next bullet from the banker's gun.

But Hardy's gun wavered, fell to his side. He made a

choking noise. His left hand clawed at his shirt collar and tore it open. As he fell both Mills and Jim saw the blood that welled out of the hole at the base of his neck. He was dead before he hit the floor.

"Gold, that's what he wanted," Tom Dolan said afterward, after they'd used three buckets of water and a bottle of spirits of ammonia to sober him to the point where he could talk coherently.

"Gold?" Nan echoed. She was in the cell with Mills, Jim, the sheriff, and the doctor who had bandaged Jim's shoulder. The sheriff had ridden down the street in time to hear the shooting, and Jim had insisted that Red's sister be called in to hear what Tom Dolan said.

The oldster nodded at the girl's unbelieving question, continuing: "Gold and lots of it! In that old test hole me and Bob Sterling sunk up at the north end of his place. If I hadn't been so damn' drunk, I wouldn't have given Hardy away tonight. Up until now I thought anyone with the name of Sterling deserved a good kick in the pants. That's what I was givin' Red when I let Hardy pay me five hundred to keep my mouth shut. Hell, I'd been workin' with Hardy for two years on this thing."

"It's my duty to warn you that anything you say will be . . . ," the sheriff started to say.

Tom Dolan waved him to silence. "I don't give a damn about that. This thing's been preyin' on my mind, and I got to git it off." He looked at Nan once more, saying: "Remember that row your old man and me had up there at the test hole?"

Nan nodded. "Right after you quit."

"That was the beginnin'," Dolan said. "Bob fancied himself quite a prospector. He wanted to work east out of the hole to try and strike the vein. We'd taken some pretty good samples out. I wanted to dig west, thinkin' the vein lay that way. We rowed about it, and I got fired about the time Bob's wife gave him hell at home. It turned out that he dynamited the hole, swearin' he'd never work it again. He didn't, neither."

"Then how did you know about the gold?" Jim asked.

Tom Dolan chuckled. "The dynamite gave me an idea. Bob used only a couple of sticks, so's not to wreck things too bad in case he ever wanted to go back to work there. I rode out one day and went down the ladder to see how much damage was done by the explosion. It had blown a hole on the west side of the shaft, my side, and laid open as pretty a quartz vein as I ever set eyes on!"

"Why didn't you tell my father?" Nan asked.

"Him!" Dolan said sourly. "Put him onto somethin' like that? Uhn-uh. Nor his son, either. I got hard up for money two or three years later and went to John Hardy with what I knew, since he held the note on the place and would get it in the end, anyway. I didn't tell him all I knew but enough so's he laid money on the line. The other night, when he gunned Withers through the office window, I was down the alley. I didn't see nothin' but I knew who'd done it. Hardy didn't want Withers to take over that note. So the next mornin', after things had quieted down some, I went to Hardy."

"Lucky he didn't kill you," Jim said.

"Not lucky, just smart. I still hadn't told him where the gold was. So he had to hand over some money. The plan was for me to fade out of the country for a while, and then come back. But I took one drink too many up there at Timberline and stayed on."

Later, as the dawn's light was lifting the shadows under the awnings along the walks on the street, Jim and Nan walked down to the hotel. Jim's right arm was in a sling. The flesh wound in his shoulder throbbed with a dull ache.

"What now, Jim?" Nan asked.

"You're rich, Nan."

She said softly: "Because of you, Jim. Will you stay?"

He smiled down at her. "I reckon I'm a cowhand. I wouldn't know a thing about minin'."

She stopped suddenly, and he was surprised at the strange look of determination on her face. "Jim, you can't leave! I don't know a thing about business affairs. And . . . and . . . I couldn't let you go anyway."

"Why not, Nan?"

"Don't you know?" Her face had taken on a deeper shade of color.

He forgot his arm and how it hurt him as he took it out of the sling. He couldn't find the right words to say. Instead, he gathered her in his arms. She let him kiss her before she gently pushed away and looked up into his eyes, saying: "Don't ever leave me, Jim. Not ever!"

Signed on Satan's Payroll

The title Jon Glidden originally gave this story was "Gun Law for a Fence-Clipper." It was completed shortly after Thanksgiving in 1937 and was sold by the author's agent to Mike Tilden, editor of *Star Western* at Popular Publications, on December 18, 1937. The author was paid $202.50. It appeared in the March, 1938 issue of *Star Western* under the title "Signed on Satan's Payroll". This title has been retained for its first appearance in book form.

I

When a man has ridden for five hours head-on into a sub zero, screeching blizzard wind, he isn't quite himself. Luke Storm wasn't himself, nor were the five others, particularly Bill Trench, their Singletree ramrod. What they'd found that morning had galled them all, including Luke. But now, as their ponies turned through the deep, powdery snow into Andy Mills's cabin yard, Luke Storm still had enough wits about him to sense that they were off on the wrong foot.

"I'd go easy on this," he told Bill Trench as he rode alongside the foreman. "I think you ought to take it in to the sheriff and let him handle it."

Bill Trench was young, lacking a year of Luke's twenty-nine, but when he pulled his chin up out of his buffalo-skin collar and turned his glance at Luke, the bleak set to his blunt features made him look much older. "What you think don't count for a damn, Storm! Keep out of this!"

Luke had invited that answer, yet it stung. As he swung into line behind Trench, he told himself for the hundredth time in his six-month stay at the Singletree outfit that he'd pull up stakes and drift. To hell with Trench and this high-riding outfit!

Just then they all heard the muted, hollow ring of an axe out back rising above the howling of the wind, and the six of them went on through the yard and across to the wagon shed. They found Andy Mills and his boy in the lee of the shed, peeling poles for a new corral. Back here, where the wind lost its force, the air seemed momentarily warm and the whine of the storm was muffled, so that when Bill Trench called softly—"Andy!"—the rancher and his youngster both turned in startled surprise.

"Howdy, gents." Andy whipped the head of his axe into the butt end of a pole and sauntered across to meet them. Then the look on Bill Trench's face stopped him. "Anything wrong?"

Trench folded his arms and leaned his stocky frame forward against the saddle horn. "Andy, you look tired. How come you don't sleep nights?"

"I don't get it, Bill. I had a good sleep last night."

"Then you got it in the saddle. Andy, we found those critters . . . bunched near your fire. We found these, too." Trench reached around and lifted two vent irons out of his saddlebag and threw them so that they fell at Andy's feet.

Andy didn't stoop to pick them up. "The last I saw of 'em they were in the woodshed out back. Where did you find 'em?"

"Lyin' in the ashes of a fire three miles north, where your range drops off into the breaks. Sixty head of our Singletree critters were yarded up in the lee of a ridge close by. We've been followin' the sign of that herd since nine this mornin'."

Young Bobby Mills had come out to stand alongside his father, his young and straight body tall for his twelve years, his rounded face and sandy hair a younger image of Andy's. He caught the meaning behind Trench's words, and now hastened to put in: "Dad wasn't out of the house all last night."

Andy said: "You keep out of this, Bob." Then he turned to Trench: "You're sayin' I stole your beef? Better go careful, Trench!"

"That's three times we've lost herds this winter," Trench told him tonelessly. "Before this we've lacked proof that it was you and the rest of these small ranchers. Now we've got it."

He straightened in his saddle and unbuttoned his sheepskin. It fell away, exposing the handle of the six-shooter at his thigh.

"Trench, that's a lie!"

Andy's words rang, clipped and hard. He seemed about to say something else, but Trench's right hand moved under his coat and whipped out a short-barreled Colt. Andy tried to get his youngster out of the way, and Luke Storm reined in alongside Trench, reaching out to knock his gun arm down. But a split second before his blow connected, the weapon beat out its hollow explosion to bring Andy stretching up on tiptoe, clawing at his chest. His face upturned, his mouth open in a soundless cry, he spun half about and fell, sending up a puff of flaky snow about his rigid frame.

A smaller flurry alongside the ramrod's horse showed where Trench's gun had fallen from the impact of Luke's down-striking blow.

Luke vaulted out of his saddle and ran over to Andy. Bobby Mills stood staring, crying hysterically: "You've killed Dad! You've killed him!"

One look at Andy was enough. Luke tore the man's canvas jacket apart and saw the matted blood on his chest, his eyes already glazing. Then, with the choked cry of Andy's boy adding fire to his rage, Luke peeled off his buffalo coat and laid it across Andy's face.

He turned to Bill Trench, drawling flatly: "Andy didn't pack a gun, Trench. Climb down and take what's comin' to you!"

Bill Trench glanced down at his weapon on the ground. Seeing that gesture, Luke reached down and unbuckled his belt and swung it and his holstered .45 far to one side.

"Don't stall, Bill. Climb down!" he said with determination.

"You're loco, Storm! Get back up and ride home."

"Don't make me come over and pull you down, Trench."

"Now, listen, Luke . . . cool off. That herd was on Andy's pasture, and those were his irons. There's no guess about it this time."

"And why would a man lift a herd of Singletree beef and leave 'em parked right under our noses? Why would he leave his irons in a brandin' fire to give him away? Why wouldn't he drive on down into the breaks where it'd take us a week to find 'em? That was murder, Trench. Are you too yellow to fight?"

That challenge was thrown in the hearing of four of Trench's men. Trench climbed out of his saddle, whipped off his coat, and sauntered the three steps that put him in front of Luke. His solid frame moved with an ease that gave clear proof of brute strength.

"You asked for it, Luke," he growled, and feinted with his right and sent a solid left smashing in at Luke's face.

Luke took the blow, turning with it and side-stepping Trench's quick rush. The Singletree ramrod came at him half bent at the waist, his fists driving up from the level of his knees. Too late, he saw Luke's tall frame dodge aside, for Luke shot in three short punches that caught Trench on the side of the jaw and spun him halfway around. Trench spread his legs, ducked his head, and met Luke's blows with a wild swinging of his fists, making no effort to protect himself. Time and again Luke's drives connected solidly, until Trench's face was bruised and bleeding.

Suddenly Trench lunged forward, caught Luke off balance, and clamped a hold above his waist with both arms. He burrowed his head down on Luke's chest and tightened that hold until Luke felt the breath sough out of his lungs and a blade of pain shoot up along his back. Then Luke felt that brute-like strength breaking him, tearing his back muscles, and crushing his chest. He tried once to drive Trench's head aside with a blow, but it only served to tighten the corded muscles about his waist.

Luke went limp, throwing his two feet out between Trench's legs so that his shifting weight overbalanced the two of them. As Trench fell forward, Luke kicked the man's right leg from under him. They landed in a turning roll, Trench on the bottom, all of Luke's hundred and seventy pounds crashing onto him. The force of the fall momentarily broke the hold, and Luke surged upward and rolled out of those massive, reaching arms.

He was on his feet again, Trench leaping up cat-like for another headlong rush. The man had tasted the feel of his strength a moment ago, and now nothing but the urge to crush Luke Storm's tall flat body drove him on. This time Luke kept out of reach, flashing in long, stabbing blows that connected solidly, time and again.

When Trench got a hold again around his waist, Luke whirled and swung the man off his feet and brought home an uppercut that sent Trench flying out to land ten feet away in the snow. Luke stood above him as he came slowly to his knees and staggered to his feet. Then, with a rhythmic, bone-crushing beat, he drove his aching fists solidly at the ramrod's face. When Trench finally fell, Luke reached down and tried to lift him to his feet again. He lacked the strength.

"That'll do, Luke," one of the riders said. He nodded to the others, and they all swung down out of their saddles. Luke stepped back warily to where his holstered gun lay in the snow and picked it up, half drawing the weapon. "It's all right with us, Luke," the rider added. "Bill had that comin'."

Luke buckled on his belt as they lifted their ramrod's unconscious bulk and threw him across his saddle.

"Shorty," Luke said, to the man who had spoken. "I've got

a razor and a couple of blankets I'll need. On your next trip into town bring the stuff along and leave it at the hotel."

"You're quittin'?"

"What do you think?" Luke tried to grin.

Shorty Bates, the tallest of the four, looked down bleakly at young Bobby Mills who knelt beside his father's body. "I'm sorry about this, kid." It was all that could be said, and Shorty, realizing it, turned away, climbed into his saddle, and led the way out of the yard.

Later, after Luke had hitched up Andy's buckboard and they were on the way to town, the boy spoke for the first time. "What I said was the truth. Dad was home all last night."

"I know, I know," Luke breathed, still held by the impotency of the beating he had given Bill Trench. "He wasn't any more to blame for it than you were. It was a frame-up."

"A frame-up?" The boy looked up at him, all the shocked grief of the past hour mirrored in his staring, bloodshot brown eyes. "But why would they do that to Dad?"

"That's what I aim to find out." Luke cast a glance back at Andy's body where it lay under the burlap sacking in the wagon bed.

"Who would do it?" the boy went on, seeming to want a direct answer. "All Dad's friends hate the Singletree, but it couldn't have been Sam Price."

"No." Luke was sure of that—it couldn't have been Sam Price. The Singletree owner, crippled so badly with rheumatism this winter that he didn't often get out of the house, had left the running of the outfit to Sue, his daughter, and to Bill Trench. Maybe, if the old man had been up and around, or if the girl had known how things were really going, this wouldn't have happened.

During the past eight months rustling had set the tempers

of this Wildcat range on edge. It had started last spring, with the disappearance of three hundred head of Singletree beef. Bill Trench had doggedly followed the lost herd's sign deep into the badlands to the north, only to lose it across a vast-stretching bed of *malpais*. Three times since then the same thing had happened, and the results had been the same. Bill Trench—already named as the man Sue Price would marry when he got together enough money to buy his own outfit—had had a hard time explaining it all to old Sam. The Singletree owner had given him a free hand to hunt out the rustlers his own way, and from that time on Bill Trench had changed.

He had hired half a dozen gun-slick killers on fighting wages and bunked them along with Shorty Bates and the few other old hands who stayed. The pastures were guarded at night all through the summer and fall, and even now, when they should have been taking it easy except in blizzard weather, the crew rode the fences once each day and slept in the line shacks. Trench himself had changed from a hard-working, good-natured wagon boss to an arrogant, brutal leader of a pack of curly wolves. Once he had guns to back him, he flatly announced that the small ranchers neighboring on the Singletree had stolen the beef. The ranchers, fearing what might happen if they called the man, had kept silent and hoped that no more Singletree herds left their home range.

Now this had happened, and Andy Mills was dead. . . . Luke thought about it all the way to town, remembering that he had been Andy's friend and that he owed something to the fatherless boy.

He didn't put his thoughts into words until they were in the cow town of Wildcat, until Sheriff Race Masters had taken young Bobby out to his house and left the youngster with Mrs. Masters.

Back in the jail office once more, the lawman's first question was: "What'll you do now, Luke? It's goin' to be pretty hot for you, with Bill Trench on the prod."

"I've seen it hotter," Luke answered. "Wonder if I hadn't ought to go back home with the kid and kind of look after him until Andy's folks arrive and straighten things up."

"I was thinkin' I'd ask him to stay with us."

Luke was silent for a full minute. Finally he flicked alight a match and touched it to his pipe, inhaling the smoke and letting it out in a gusty sigh. "You don't know me very well, do you, Masters?"

"You've been here less than a year, Luke."

"Andy Mills was my friend. I rode that fence past his place all summer and got to know him. He didn't have a chance against Bill Trench. He wasn't even wearin' a gun. I think I'll stay."

Masters was a man past middle age. He had spent fifteen years wearing a law badge, had seen enough so that the pattern of today's happenings was an old one. He lifted his sloping shoulders in a shrug. "These things happen, Luke. Bill found the evidence. Maybe he was hasty, maybe he shouldn't have pulled his iron on Andy. But the law has a way of dealin' with rustlers, and it'll back Bill Trench in what he did. It won't do you any good to stay."

"You mean that Sam Price can make his own law just because he's a big man in this country. You mean the law will overlook a murder because of that."

Masters shrugged again. "If puttin' it that way suits you any better, then, yes."

"I'll still stay."

"And what good will it do you?"

"I'll find out who stole the beef."

Masters shook his head emphatically. "Luke, I've spent

the last eight months tryin' to find that out. You'll only buy yourself trouble, and, if you do, I can't help you."

"That's my look-out. I . . . ," Luke's words broke off as the office door opened.

In the opening stood a girl. She was tall, with the collar of a dark brown wool jacket turned up about her neck. Her aquiline face, flushed from the cold, showed a severe set that gave only a hint of beauty. Sue Price could be beautiful, Luke was thinking as he got up out of his chair and nodded to her, but now a certain grimness of expression gave her features strength rather than good looks.

"I came as soon as I heard," she said as she closed the door behind her. "Where is Bobby Mills?"

"I took him to the house, Sue," Masters told her.

"I'll have to go see him." Then, looking at Luke, her blue eyes took on a fire. "I brought your things in with me, Luke. They're out in the buckboard. Here's your pay."

She held out an envelope, and he took it without comment.

"Don't you have anything to say, Luke?"

"Only that I wish I'd done a better job on Trench."

Her eyes were blazing with anger now. "Of course, I'm sorry it happened. But it was no call for you to act like . . . like a. . . ."

"Like a man who's just seen a friend murdered," Luke supplied her words.

"But Bill found proof of what Andy had done!"

"Then why didn't he bring Andy in to the sheriff? Why didn't he . . . ?" Luke ended his words abruptly, weary of voicing a pointless argument.

Sue Price had driven to town to do what she could for Andy's boy, but believing what Bill Trench had probably told her—that Andy was as guilty as any man who ever breathed.

"I didn't expect this of you, Luke Storm! I thought you knew what we were up against . . . that Dad has lost nearly six hundred head to rustlers these last eight months. And now that we find out who's responsible . . . simply because Bill Trench lost his head because of months of worry . . . you act like a common saddle tramp!"

"Andy didn't even have a gun."

"And I suppose you think he deserved a fair chance . . . after what he'd done?"

Luke didn't answer for a long moment. But when he spoke he had carefully thought out what he would say: "Andy deserved more then he got . . . which was no chance at all. I think someone framed him, and I aim to be here to see that the man who did it gets exactly the same chance as Andy . . . none at all."

Seeing the quick anger that took possession of the girl, Race Masters hastened to put in: "Sue, if I was you, I'd get on up to the house and see the boy. Try and tell him. . . ."

"Try not to tell him you think his dad was a rustler," Luke said.

The girl raked him with a loathing glance and went out the door, slamming it behind her.

"You're hard on her, Luke. You can't blame her for the way she feels."

"I don't blame anyone for anything . . . except Trench for what he did. Maybe before long I can bring you something that'll make you and the rest throw away your blinders, Sheriff."

II

The full force of the blizzard struck early the next afternoon, with the wind blowing a gale, the temperature dropping, and snow. Even so, twenty-two people came to the cemetery to hear Parson Elford's shouted words whipped away unheard in the whine of the wind, to see the new pine coffin lowered by ropes into the frozen, snow-drifted grave.

When two men with shovels stepped forward to fill in the grave, the frozen clods of dirt thumping hollowly on the coffin's new yellow boards, Andy's boy reached out and took Luke's hand. He looked up at him and said: "You aren't going to leave, are you, Luke?"

"We'll drive on out home before dark," Luke told him, trying to keep the huskiness out of his voice.

Afterward, while motherly Mrs. Masters took the youngster home with her to get him some warm clothes and to heat some bricks to put under his feet on the long ride back to the cabin, Luke and a few others turned in at Ed Emmerson's bar for a drink of whiskey to thaw them out. Across the street, half a dozen Singletree bronchos stood down-headed at the tie-rail in front of the Melodian, Bradley King's saloon.

Months ago, after Bill Trench had named the small ranches as rustlers, Andy Mills and his friends had stopped patronizing Brad King's Melodian, wisely choosing to keep out of the way of the Singletree crew. In Ed Emmerson's place across the street they found a quieter hang-out, for Emmerson didn't hire faro and poker dealers and his only bartender didn't wear a white coat. When a drunk started raising the roof, he was thrown out.

Steve Merritt, Andy's nearest neighbor to the south, came

in with Luke, nodding toward the Singletree ponies across the street. "Trench and a few of his hardcases are bellyin' the bar across there."

That was Trench's way, Luke was thinking, to ride in through the storm today and be on hand in case anyone started the wrong kind of talk about the way he had settled things with Andy Mills.

Steve Merritt had something more to say. "Take a look down the bar and see who's here."

Luke glanced toward the back of the room and saw Shorty Bates's high-built frame propped against the end of the bar. No one stood close to the Singletree rider. It was plain that he was unwelcome here, but he stood there fingering a shot glass in apparent unconcern. When he met Luke's glance, he forced a wry smile. They were friends, and had been ever since Luke joined up with the outfit.

Luke went on back and stood alongside Shorty.

"Have a drink?" Luke asked.

Shorty shook his head. "Not now, Luke, not because I don't want to, but because I want to get out of this place. In another five minutes one of these jaspers will have worked up the guts to invite me out. I'm glad you came."

"Why aren't you across the street?"

"I should be, but there's something I wanted to tell you. Trench is on the prod. His face looks like a range bull had bedded down on it. If he can get you alone, he'll make a try at you . . . with guns. Why don't you head out of the country?"

"Thanks, Shorty, but there's things to do here first . . . such as findin' out who drove that herd onto Andy's range."

Shorty was thoughtful for a moment, finally nodding. "I reckon I'd feel the same way. How do you aim to do it?"

Luke shrugged and kept his silence.

"What I came to tell you is this, friend," Shorty said. "In

case you run into anything that looks queer, let me know. Me and a couple of the others have taken about as much from Bill Trench as we're goin' to. What happened yesterday has got the bunkhouse pretty well divided out there. It wouldn't take a lot to make a few of us pull out."

"Thanks, Shorty. I didn't know you felt that way about Bill."

Shorty hitched up his trousers and stepped back from the bar and said: "Neither did I . . . until yesterday." He looked up along the bar at the others, noticing the way they were looking at him. "I reckon I can make it to the front door without trouble."

After the door slammed behind the man's tall frame, silence held the room, until Luke said: "It's here, gents."

Men turned to face him as he spoke—Steve Merritt, Roy Messar, Bill Foley, One-Eye Jamison, Flint McCauley.

It was Flint McCauley, whose outfit lay ten miles east of the Singletree, who queried curtly: "What's here?"

Luke stepped out from the bar. He walked over to a table and leaned against it so that he faced them directly. "Trench is through fiddlin' around. When the storm breaks, he aims to do a little ridin'. You're one of the gents he figures to call on, Flint." Luke gave the lie flatly, knowing that this was the only way of prodding these men into bunching their strength.

"A hell of a lot of good it'll do him!" Flint blazed. He was a big, powerful, middle-aged man who had worked up from a forty-a-month cowpuncher to the owner of a sixteen-section outfit. It had taken him twenty years to achieve his small success, and he would fight for what his brains and brawn had given him.

Luke said: "Some of you think Andy got what he deserved. Maybe you ought to check out while the rest of us who were Andy's friends make our medicine."

Luke was looking at Bill Foley, and the man's glance wavered and fell before his hard stare. He had singled out Foley as the weakest link in this chain, the least likely to fight if it came to a showdown, because he lived farthest from the Singletree. "You, Foley. You're in the same saddle as the rest of us. What do you say?"

"I want to know what's bringin' you in on this!" Foley said. "You're a stranger here, and now you start somethin' none of us can finish. Or if it ever is finished, we'll see the Singletree crowdin' us out! Why can't you let things stay as they are? I'm gettin' along all right."

Steve Merritt put in: "If a rattler crawls under your blankets, you don't lie there waitin' for him to strike, do you, Bill? As far as Luke's concerned, he was Andy's friend. He beat hell out of Bill Trench yesterday, which is more than I'd have the guts to take on. If that don't buy him into our game, what could?"

A chorus of divided sentiment met his words, but, surprisingly, the greatest number sided with Bill Foley. Not that they distrusted Luke, for there was little doubt but what he was with them, but they were wary of forcing a fight against the Singletree. Bill Foley and a few others, finding that they weren't alone in their opinions, flatly refused to listen to any hasty decision.

"Let's wait and give Bill Trench a chance to cool down," Foley suggested, when he could make himself heard above the din. "I don't think Andy stole those critters, Storm. But so long as they let me alone, I'm not startin' a fight. If this happens again, maybe I'll listen, but, until it does, I'm workin' my own range and mindin' my own business."

"It'll happen again," Luke told him. "And when it does . . . the next time another herd strays off Singletree pasture . . . I aim to know who drives it and where it goes."

"How'll you find that out?" Steve Merritt queried.

"You've got a four man outfit, Steve. Flint works five. Each of you can spare two men. Countin' me, that'll make five men who can start ridin' Singletree fence at dark tomorrow. Every time a herd has disappeared, it's gone out at night through the Singletree's east fence. Five men can ride that fence pretty well. We can keep under cover and still know what goes on. If another herd is stolen, we'll know about it within an hour of the time it happens. And with five men, we can follow the herd and put up a good scrap if it comes to a showdown. I don't know who's behind this, but that's one way of findin' out."

Bill Foley, his friends now grouped around him, said: "Count me out. I stay set until I have a damned good reason to change my mind!" He turned around, drained a half inch of whiskey from his shot glass at the bar, and growled—"I'm through with this nonsense!"—and went out the door up front.

Singly, and in pairs, the ones who went with him followed. Finally Steve Merritt and the two men of his crew who had ridden in with him, along with Flint McCauley and one of his cowpunchers, were alone at the bar with Luke.

Steve sighed his disgust and said: "There goes our fight! All we can do now is run when Bill Trench barks. Foley's got twelve miles of range between his lay-out and the Singletree. And he's so ornery he won't budge now that his mind is made up."

"Then we'll have to try to swing it alone," Luke told him.

That night Luke built a roaring fire in the hogback stove in Andy's cabin, and he and the boy cooked a meal and ate it in silence.

Finally, after the dishes were finished and they had taken

chairs close to the stove and Luke had lit his pipe, Bobby said: "Sue Price told me she was sorry about Dad. She's nice. She wanted me to come and live with them at the Singletree."

"What did you tell her?"

"I told her I thought you were going to stay with me."

"How come, Bobby? I hadn't said anything about it."

Bobby gave a quick shrug of his narrow shoulders. "I don't know. I just knew you would after what you did to Bill Trench. She asked me about that."

"About the fight?"

The boy nodded. "She asked me all about it. About what Dad said and about the way Bill Trench . . . the way he shot Dad. I told her, and she wanted me to tell you she was sorry for the way she acted in the sheriff's office."

Luke smiled thinly, for the moment taking a grim satisfaction in realizing that Sue Price had learned the real story from the boy and that she had fought down her pride enough to admit her mistake. Perhaps, in finding the truth, she would be curious enough to open her eyes to a few things that were going on around the Singletree—to see that Bill Trench was riding a little too high, that he had hired the type of men old Sam Price had never tolerated on his payroll. Maybe she'd lose a little of her respect for Bill Trench and discover before it was too late the kind of a husband he would make her.

"Did she have anything else to say?"

"She wanted to know all about what Dad had been doing the last few days. I couldn't tell her. He's been in town a lot . . . I don't know why."

Luke's interest was immediately aroused. In the spell of weather they'd had for the past few weeks, it was strange that Andy would leave the snug warmth of the cabin for more than one trip to town.

"He went in mostly afternoons and nights and only took

me along once, the last time," the boy continued. "It was night before last."

Luke leaned forward in his chair. "Try to remember what he did, Bob. Where did he go? How long did he stay?"

The boy frowned. "It was real late. We drove in after supper to get bailing wire for the new corral. Dad went in Harvey's store and came back after a while with a few things he put in the buckboard. Then he told me he had to see a man and for me to go into the hotel if I got too cold. It took him a long time, and I went into the hotel and waited while he went into the Melodian Bar."

Luke shifted forward in his chair, intent on what he had to say. "The Melodian, eh? Andy didn't often go there, did he?"

The boy looked puzzled. "That's right . . . not for a long time. But he did the other night," he insisted. "About midnight, Harry Badger, the clerk, woke me up and told me he was lockin' up. So I went into the saloon and found him. He and two other men were at the bar signing that big sheet of paper."

"A sheet of paper?" Luke searched his memory to discover what the boy might mean. Finally he had it. "You mean the Christmas turkey raffle?"

Bob nodded. "That's it. On the way home Dad said we might have a real feast on Christmas Day." Remembering that, tears welled into the boy's eyes, but he swallowed hard and wiped his eyes with the back of one hand and waited for Luke's next question.

"Who was it that Andy was talking to, Bob?"

"I couldn't see. They had their backs to me and both wore buffalo coats."

"Were they tall or short? What did they look like?" Luke sat tensely, knowing that much depended on the boy's answer.

But Bob finally shook his head haltingly. "I . . . I just can't remember."

Luke sat back in his chair, suddenly gone limp at the implications behind the news the boy had given him. Andy Mills at the Melodian, talking to two men, letting his youngster wait for him alone in the cold for hours!

Abruptly Luke got up out of the chair and went to the door and took down his coat and put it on.

"Where are you goin', Luke?" the boy asked.

"I'll be back before long, son. You put a chunk of wood in the stove before you go to bed. And don't stay up too late." Luke was busy tying a bandanna tightly around his ears below the rim of his Stetson. As he reached for the door latch, he turned all at once to face the boy. "Bob, did you tell all this to the girl . . . to Sue Price?"

"Only about Dad driving to town. I didn't remember the rest until just now when you asked me about it."

III

Reining in at the nearly empty tie rail in front of the Melodian, Luke was thankful the weather had not let up. His hands were numb and his face nearly frozen, but he welcomed the discomfort in the knowledge that the Melodian would be doing a poor business tonight.

He examined the brands on the four ponies standing along the awninged walk. Only one bore the jaw brand of the Singletree, another thing that was comforting. On any night in good weather he would have found at least half a dozen Singletree riders in the Melodian. He wasn't exactly anxious to meet any of them now.

The ride had taken him two full hours. It was past eleven, and, as he pulled the storm door shut behind him and stepped into the warm stale air of the saloon, he counted only five customers, four of them at the table closest to the potbellied stove in the room's center.

Shorty Bates stood alone at the bar, talking to the bartender. "Look who's here!" Shorty drawled. "You can buy me that drink I wouldn't take this afternoon, Luke. How come you're up so late?"

Luke answered briefly. "I don't know yet." He flipped a silver dollar onto the counter.

After they had downed their drinks, Luke shook his broad shoulders and unbuckled his buffalo coat. "Now I feel human," he drawled. "This is good Christmas weather, eh?" He turned to the barman. "How's the raffle comin', Tom?"

"A little over a hundred and forty chances at five dollars a throw. Not bad," Tom conceded.

"Five dollars is big money to pay for a turkey."

"Not when it's buyin' winter grub for those starvin' miners up in the hills," Shorty Bates put in. "I think it's a damned good idea. Saves the county money."

"Maybe you're right." Luke chuckled, reaching into his pocket. He counted his change and found himself a quarter short of five dollars. "Make me a loan, Shorty, since you're feelin' so charitable. Tom, bring out your sheet and let me sign. I wouldn't mind turkey for Christmas."

Shorty supplied the missing quarter while Tom went on back to get the big white poster leaning against the back end of the bar mirror. He laid it on the counter in front of Luke. "We're workin' on the back side now. You got a pencil, Luke?"

Luke didn't answer. He had picked up the cardboard sheet and turned it over and was casually running a finger down the list of names on the front when Shorty Bates suddenly put in: "Hurry up and write down your handle, Luke. I'm buyin' this drink."

But Luke didn't hurry. His eyes scanned the first column without finding Andy Mills's name. He didn't look up at Shorty, but he sensed that the man's reaction had something to do with what he was about to discover.

Toward the bottom of the second column he found Andy's name, Andrew Mills, scrawled in a jerky hand. Above Andy's name he read, William Trench, above that a strange name that meant nothing to him. But below, written in a neat, precise hand, was Shorty Bates, and below Shorty's he found the name of the town banker, Ford Stephens.

He timed his movements to an agonizing slowness as he reversed the poster and carefully signed his name below the last entry.

"I'll take that drink now, Shorty."

Bates laid a half dollar on the counter. Luke didn't look at

112

him, thinking he might give himself away.

A minute later, after the raw taste of the whiskey had mellowed in his mouth, he asked: "Tom, who was the first gent to sign this thing yesterday mornin'?" He let his right hand go down to rest easily on his upraised thigh, his right foot on the polished foot rail. The butt of his holstered six-gun was within finger spread reach of his hand.

Tom scratched his head and frowned. "I remember now. It was old man Stephens. Goddlemighty, but it was good to see him dig down into that moldy old purse and count out five bucks in chicken feed! I bet it hurts him to write his name. Why you askin', Luke?"

"Just an idea," Luke answered, raising his glance to regard Shorty, but he found the man staring absently at his folded hands on the bar top.

"This is pretty late for a family man to be stayin' out," he said a minute later. "Let me know how things are goin', Shorty."

There was nothing in Shorty's half smiling glance that betrayed even a hint of veiled emotion. Luke felt immediately relieved. The man didn't suspect what he had been doing, after all. He climbed into his saddle out front and set out along the west trail at a stiff trot.

What he had discovered that night was hard to believe. Bill Trench's name on the list directly above Andy's—and Shorty Bates's immediately below! To read those two names had frozen something within him that even Shorty's whiskey hadn't thawed. Andy's visit there at the bar had taken him probably two or three hours, and all that time Andy had been in the Melodian, talking to Bill Trench and Shorty Bates, men who were supposed to be unfriendly to him. What had been Andy's business with those two?

Suddenly he thought he knew. A herd had been found on

Andy's range the day following. Who had discovered the theft of that herd? Shorty Bates! He had reported it early in the morning, and Bill Trench had taken five men and set out in the teeth of a blizzard to find that herd.

Looking back at it now, Luke could see things he hadn't noticed that morning. For instance, Bill Trench had unerringly followed the sign through wind-whipped, drifting snow that would have defeated even an Indian's keen eye. Luke had given the man credit for having more than average experience at reading sign. Now he knew that Trench hadn't read it at all. He'd simply known where to find that herd.

"Bill and Shorty planted that beef on Andy's pasture," he said aloud. "They framed him!"

Knowing that for a fact, he was amazed at the implications in the discovery. Beef had been stolen from the Singletree four other times during the past eight months. Couldn't Bill Trench have stolen it those other times in the same way to frame Andy? Why frame Andy Mills?—*Because he was in with Trench, and because Trench was through using him.* The answer came logically, lacking only definite proof. Bill Trench had stolen herds from the man he was working for, driven them down into the breaks himself, or turned them over to Andy to drive for him. Why? Because he needed money. Wasn't it common knowledge that Trench would marry Sue Price when he had saved enough to buy his own outfit?

The only thing that wouldn't fit into the puzzle was Shorty Bates's place in the scheme. Shorty had come to work for the Singletree the same month Luke had signed on, last June. There must be things about Shorty that Luke didn't know. He had been friendly with Bill Trench, that much Luke knew for sure. But today, after the funeral, Shorty had come into Ed Emmerson's place, in front of all those hostile small ranchers, and named himself as their friend. Was Shorty trying to throw up a blind and win the confidence of the men who might someday be fighting against Bill Trench? It looked like it. *And he knows now!* Luke reasoned. Shorty had known what Luke's visit to the Melodian meant, after all. He had known the reason behind Luke's questioning the bartender about the first signer of the raffle sheet the morning after Andy's visit.

Wariness flooded through Luke Storm in a wave that immediately sent his glance back along the trail. As far as he could see into the snow-lit darkness, he was alone. Then his glance shuttled up the slope along which he was riding.

Sixty yards of open, white-mantled ground lay between him and a fringe of stunted cedars that capped the crest of the hill to his right. A man could hide up there and get a clean shot at him. Shorty could have followed, circled the trail, and forted up on that crest.

At that precise moment he saw the orange wink of powder flame that pinpointed the darkness at the margin of the trees. Instinctively he sloped forward in the saddle, hearing the brittle *crack* of the rifle as he moved. Then a slamming blow hit him solidly in his right shoulder, knocking him sideways. The gelding shied, reared onto his hind legs, and Luke's instinct made him drop the reins and roll out of the saddle on the off side.

The trail sloped steeply down on his left. He hit with a hard, shoulder-wrenching jolt and rolled down off the trail, half protected by the bank above. His first impulse was to reach for the holstered six-gun at his thigh. But wariness cautioned him against it. He would make too good a target for the bushwhacker if he moved. Luke had no doubt but that it was Shorty.

He lay quietly, moving slightly to ease the strain on his right shoulder that already throbbed with pain. The minutes dragged on, while he muted even his breathing in the hope of catching some sound. The man might come down to make sure his bullet had done its work. In that case Luke would have to trust to his hearing to give him warning.

Once or twice he heard his pony moving a few yards below on the trail. But that was the only sound that came to him through the crisp, cold air. Then, shuttling clearly across from the slope above, he heard the sound of a breaking branch, then the rhythmic hoof beats of a trotting horse. He lay still, gauging the sound, ten seconds later feeling a weakness settle through him as the sound receded.

It was two minutes before the far mutter of that hoof pound faded into the night's utter silence. Still he lay there, knowing that to move now might betray him, thinking of Shorty, of Andy Mills, and of Bill Trench. Bill had used Andy and had finished with him. It was Shorty and Bill now.

Five minutes later he got stiffly to his feet, stepped carefully up the bank, and walked the twenty yards to where his gelding was standing. Shorty had been sure that his bullet had done the work. Otherwise he wouldn't have gone on.

Luke stood thoughtfully for one long minute, reasoning that the logical thing to do was to keep out of sight for the time being. Only in that way—thinking Luke dead and knowing that their secret was still safe—would Bill Trench and Shorty make a move.

They're in this for the money, Luke told himself. *And with snow falling every day, it's good weather for swinging a sticky loop.*

It was four miles to Andy's cabin. Luke climbed into the saddle and walked the gelding a quarter mile, reining him first to one side of the trail, then to the other, so that if anyone was interested later in following the sign it would appear that the sorrel had wandered aimlessly. Then he found what he wanted—a flat, low outcropping where the wind had whipped the rock clean of snow.

He reined in alongside and climbed out of the saddle and onto the bare rock, still keeping a hold on the ribbons. Feeling the sticky warmth of the blood that was wetting his shirt, he took his right arm out of the sleeve of his coat and with his left hand smeared blood on the gelding's withers and across the saddle horn. Then he carefully broke the reins at hoof length, slapped the animal across the rump, and watched him wander off down the trail. He would head for the Singletree, his home corral.

Luke bandaged the shoulder as best he could, first moving it and making sure that no bones were broken. Then, cutting at right angles from the outcropping, he climbed the slope behind and headed northwest for the cabin. It took him four hours to make the walk. Once he stopped long enough to gather some sticks and build a fire. He took off his boots and warmed his feet, and then went on.

When he came across the yard and up to the cabin door, weakness made him walk in a spraddle-legged stride. But as he opened the door, he felt the first flakes of snow begin to fall out of the graying sky. He smiled grimly. In another two hours any sign he had left would be buried in fresh snow. He was satisfied.

He spent half an hour stoking up the stove and boiling water so that he could cleanse the wound. The bullet had narrowly missed the joint, obliquely entering the muscle below and coming out clean four inches behind it. He worked quietly so as not to wake the boy in the next room.

Finally he turned in, too weary to take off his clothes.

IV

Sue Price was working over some of her father's accounts in the ranch office early the next afternoon when she heard the shouting outside. She went onto the wide porch and saw three men of the crew down near the corral, trying to corner a riderless sorrel.

"Bring down a rope!" one of them shouted to a fourth, watching from the bunkhouse doorway.

Something familiar about the sorrel brought Sue Price down off the porch. She walked toward the corral, unmindful of the cold or the bite of the wind in her face.

By the time she had arrived at the corral, one of the crew had a rope on the animal and he and his companions were examining the saddle. Absorbed in their task, they did not notice her.

"It's Luke's, sure as hell!"

"There's some blood here."

"Blood? Give me a look." The speaker reached up to wipe his hand across the saddle horn. "Frozen." He saw a dark smear across the animal's withers, and wiped his hand across it. The hand came away bloody. His face went stone sober. "Someone go get Bill Trench."

They saw Sue then and stepped aside when she came up and looked. "You're sure this was Luke Storm's pony?" she asked.

"There ain't a doubt about it, Miss Price. That's his sorrel . . . that's his hull."

They waited while Bill Trench came down from the house. He nodded curtly to Sue. Shorty Bates came down from the bunkhouse and joined the group.

118

"Has something happened to Luke?" Sue asked Trench.

The ramrod's bruised, still handsome face took on a twisted smile. "Sort of looks that way, doesn't it?"

"I want you to have every man you can spare saddle up and work the trails. Follow this sorrel's sign as far as you can. See if you can tell where Luke was riding when it happened."

Trench's brows came up in mock surprise. "And why should we spend time lookin' after that *hombre?*"

"Bill, you'll do as I say! Get out and look for Luke."

She turned and walked back to the house, in a hot rage at Bill Trench's smugness. Last night she'd had it out with Bill, giving him the story of the shooting as Andy's boy had given it to her. He had hotly accused her of taking Luke Storm's story against his, and to see him so resentful was the beginning of her loss of respect for him. It showed her one other thing— that she had always liked Luke Storm—and now she was sincerely worried about him.

Three hours after the crew had ridden out to look for Luke, the first pairs of riders began drifting in, finished with their search. She saw Shorty come in through the yard, climb the porch, and head for the door of Bill Trench's office. Shorty was probably bringing news, so she headed down the hallway between the bedrooms for Trench's office, at the far end of the passageway.

The carpeting muffled the sound of her steps. She heard the door to Trench's office open and close; she heard Shorty stomp the snow off his boots. As her hand reached out for the knob on the door, she paused.

"He's not where I left him last night, Bill," came Shorty's voice.

"The hell he isn't! I thought you said your slug hit him in the chest!"

In the following silence, Sue's hand edged down to her side and her body tensed in fear and despair over what they were saying had happened to Luke Storm.

Bill Trench's fist suddenly banged the desk top. "Maybe I made a mistake in switchin' from Andy Mills to you. When I told Andy to do a thing, it was done right. He handled four herds for me, made 'em disappear into thin air! Now you fumble the first job I give you!"

"Easy on that talk, Bill. Storm's dead, I tell you. Only his body's been moved."

"I'll believe that when I see him wearin' a pine nightshirt." Trench paused, cursing softly, a scowl on his battered face. Then: "Well, this means we'll have to wait."

"Why? I tell you we don't have anything to worry about from Storm."

Trench cleared his throat nervously. "Where's the girl?"

"What about her? You want money for her, don't you? This is your chance. I tell you Tim Ord isn't goin' to wait much longer. We've got to get a herd over to him or he pulls out on the deal."

"We'll make the drive next week."

"Why wait? Why not tonight? You losin' your guts, Bill?"

There was a short, potent silence. Then Trench's voice droned flatly: "Losin' my guts, eh? I'll call that, Shorty! We'll see who's got the guts and who hasn't. Tonight we make the drive. You're to take over the herd outside the east fence and head it across the breaks to Ord. It'll take you two days. In case anyone asks where you and your men are, I'll tell 'em you're huntin' for Luke Storm. And if you don't come back with the money, I'll come after you!"

"Why so proddy, Bill?" came Shorty's smooth drawl. "All I wanted was to get you up off the seat of your pants."

"Get goin'!" was Trench's curt reply.

Sue Price tiptoed down the hall and into her room and sagged wearily onto her bed. What she had learned in those five minutes left little to her imagination. Andy Mills had been guilty, after all—framed by the man he had worked for, Bill Trench. The Singletree ramrod had been stealing from his own outfit and had probably thrown Andy to one side in favor of Shorty. The conversation had implied that Shorty had discovered an outlet for the stolen herds through a man named Ord who lived beyond the breaks, two days' ride from the Singletree. It was a perfect plan. In some way Luke Storm had suspected what was going on, but he was out of the way now, probably dead.

But was Luke dead, if Shorty couldn't find him? With that flicker of hope glowing to life within her, Sue got up off the bed and put on her jacket and gloves and started for the door. If Luke was alive, she'd find him. He was the only one who could help her now. Her father believed so implicitly in Bill Trench that he would probably take Trench's denial at its face value if Sue revealed what she knew. Luke was her only chance.

Outside, the quick dusk was deepening. As she came onto the ranch house porch, intending to go down to the stables and have her mare saddled, she saw Trench standing in his office doorway. He didn't see her as she drew back into the shadows. Then she went back into the house, knowing that she must let him ride away from the lay-out before she could hope to go without his seeing her. She took off her coat and gloves again, and sat down in the spacious living room before the warmth of the fire.

In twenty minutes Trench came into the room and curtly announced: "I'm headin' for the north line cabin with four men, Sue. Whoever took that last herd is liable to try again, and I don't aim to be caught flat-footed this time. I'll ride the east fence comin' home just to make sure it hasn't been cut. I'll be back late."

She didn't bother to answer him, and a moment later heard him go back to his office. She went to a darkened window and presently saw him ride away. Five minutes later she was in her saddle, heading straight east toward Andy Mills's cabin.

Five miles to the east, in the cabin, Luke Storm was telling his story to Steve Merritt and the others. Steve and Flint McCauley had ridden in half an hour ago with three men, ready to carry out Luke's plan of guarding the Singletree's east fence. They were listening soberly as he finished telling of what had happened the night before: "I came back here and fixed up the arm. Today they've probably found out they didn't get me. But they'll move fast now, if my guess is right."

"How did you find out all this?" Merritt asked.

"Something the kid told me about what Andy said the day before they got him," Luke lied, not wanting to let them know of Andy Mills's mysterious part in this. "I think Andy suspected something. That's probably why Trench framed him and killed him."

"So it's Trench and Shorty Bates," Flint mused, half aloud. He looked across at Luke with his blue eyes dully lighted in anger. "Do you want me to ride back to the lay-out and get the rest of my crew?"

"There's no time," Luke told him. "We'd better work in pairs, each taking a two-mile stretch of fence. It may not happen tonight or for several days. But it will soon. In case any of you spot anything, one man is to stay and watch what happens while the other rides to round up the rest of us. Now let's get started."

Before they went out, Luke took the boy aside. "Remember, Bob, if anyone stops by here tonight and asks for me, you're to say I've been gone since last night. No one's to know I'm alive, and you know why. Warm up some of that stew and get to bed early. And don't worry."

The boy nodded, and Luke joined the others out front. It took them the better part of an hour to reach the Singletree fence. Luke and Flint were to guard the stretch closest to the cabin. The rest went on.

They waited an hour, then Luke said: "We'd better swing north and have a look, Flint." As they went up into the saddles and started out along the four-wire fence, Luke noticed that the sky was clearing. For the first time in six days there was a hint of the new moon shining through the foggy clouds, and tonight a man could see plainly for nearly a quarter mile across the snow-lighted distance.

Less than half a mile after they had started, they saw a rider streak up out of a shallow coulée ahead and come toward them at a full run. It was one of Steve Merritt's men. He drew rein alongside Luke.

"A big herd, Luke . . . a hell of a big herd . . . just drove through the fence four miles above. Steve sent me back to tell you."

The three of them raked the flanks of their ponies and ran hard for a half hour along the line of the fence. Abruptly they came to a broad, dirty swath cut across the snow at right angles to the fence.

"There's where they came through," Merritt's man said. "I reckon Steve and the others followed."

It worked out that way. They had followed the herd's sign for only ten minutes before they saw riders ahead. They circled and, from a clump of trees along the trail, recognized Steve and the rest, and rode down and joined them.

123

"There must be four hundred head and more," Steve told them. "Shorty Bates was there, and I recognized Warren, that new hardcase Bill Trench hired a month ago. What do you figure to do, Luke?"

"With six men we can circle that herd and wait up ahead and knock every rider they've got out of the saddle before he knows what hit him. With luck, we can finish this before they reach the breaks."

Luke sent one man ahead to sight the herd. He gave him a five minute start, and then signaled the others.

In the night's half light, Sue Price stopped before Andy Mills's cabin. She saw the trampled yard in front and wondered who had stopped. She knocked on the door, and, after a moment, it opened and Andy's boy stood in the opening.

"Is Luke here?" she queried.

He shook his head, but his expression betrayed him. She stepped inside, saw that she had interrupted his meal. Only one plate of food was laid out on the table.

She took him by the shoulders and looked down at him, suddenly feeling that she must know the truth. "Bobby, I'm Luke's friend. Believe that. I want to know what happened to him, where he is now."

"He went away last night and didn't come back." He paused, his glance flinching as it met hers. Then something in her eyes told him that the girl had spoken the truth when she called herself Luke's friend, and he blurted out his story.

"He and the others have been gone an hour, ridin' east fence. Luke was hurt last night, hurt bad, but he wouldn't stay at home when the others wanted him to. He's with them."

Her grip tightened on his shoulders so that it made him wince. "They're out there, Bob? I've found out who did this

124

. . . Bill Trench and Shorty Bates. There're stealing another herd tonight . . . and, if Luke and the rest should meet them, they'll be killed. I'm going out after them."

She was halfway through the door when she heard his steps behind her. She turned, found that he'd picked up his coat and cap, and was coming with her. "You mustn't come, Bob. There may be trouble. You'll be safer here."

"But you can't go out there alone."

"Who would possibly want to hurt me?" Her laugh immediately eased his concern. "Now, you stay here, Bob, and I promise to ride back this way and tell you what happened."

He stayed in the doorway, watching her ride from the yard. He waited until the sound of the mare's hoofs had died into the distance, then went quickly out to the wagon shed. He threw a blanket over the black's back, and untied the hackamore from the ring of the feed bin. Back in the cabin, he took down his father's Colt .38 from behind the stove. Outside again, and following the mare, he kicked the black's flanks with his short legs and leaned low over the animal's back.

Sue angled west toward the fence and sighted it twenty minutes after she had left the cabin. She followed it north, so impatient that she used her spurs each time the mare showed signs of lagging. The snow made the going hard, but tonight she spared neither herself nor the animal, and a half hour later she sighted the break in the fence.

Here was unmistakable evidence of the herd's passage. She wheeled the mare and followed the sign, then, when she had gone less than a hundred yards, she heard the sound of running horses behind. She turned in the saddle to see a group of riders swinging through the broad opening in the fence. She drew rein and turned, her spirits immediately rising at the thought that this would be Luke and his friends.

But then she saw one rider cut out ahead of the rest, and, as she recognized the stocky shape in the saddle of the rangy gray, terror rode through her. She reined the mare about and slashed her spurs along the animal's flanks. Bill Trench rode a gray.

For long seconds she was sure she was holding her lead until, at the limits of her vision, a shape rode alongside.

Bill Trench reached out, caught one rein, and pulled the mare to a stop.

"Let me go!" she blazed. "Take your hands off my reins!"

But he didn't release his hold and his smile wasn't pleasant. "So you're in on this, too?" he muttered. "I wonder how you found it out."

Someone behind gave a shout. She looked back and counted three men coming up behind with a fourth farther back and to one side of the herd's trail. This fourth rider was bent low in his saddle, examining the ground. As she looked, he straightened suddenly, shouted again, and rode toward them.

"Shorty's got a pack followin' him, boss," the man announced as he rode in close to Trench. "Six of 'em. They swung after the herd from the south. The sign's fresh."

The muscles along Trench's jaw corded. He looked keenly at Sue Price, then said curtly: "Tie her into her saddle."

Two men swung down and came over to Sue. One of them reached up to take hold of her arm, while the other flicked out the looped end of the rope he had taken from his saddle. Sue jerked her hand from the man's grasp. "You can't do this to me, Bill Trench! Let me go!"

"Tie her up."

Sue fought them and kept them from getting a rope on her feet until a third man came over to help. Then her boots were laced under the mare's belly, and her hands tied to the saddle horn. Trench had knotted the end of a rope to the mare's reins, and now he took the lead, the others falling in behind as they followed the herd's trail.

From the sheltering darkness of a clump of poplars back along the fence, young Bobby Mills had witnessed this. He couldn't recognize any of the riders, but from what the girl had told him he knew that it was Bill Trench.

For the first time in his life real hatred was born within him—hatred of Bill Trench, his father's killer. His small boy's anger wiped away any trace of fear he would have felt at another time as he followed the riders into the darkness ahead. He had seen Sue Price fight them, and now that was only one more reason for hating Bill Trench.

Once, after an hour behind them, he lost sight of their shadows in the cobalt distance. So he kicked at the black and rode faster, pulling the animal into its steady trot only when he had them in sight again.

A moment later, the far thunder of guns beat dully out of the distance. He saw the line of riders ahead stop suddenly, then they spread out and went on at a run. He swung wide of the trail and bent low along the black's back as he took out after them.

V

They had picked a perfect spot for the ambush. Circling ahead of the cattle, they had found a mile-long, narrow draw that led down into the breaks, directly in the path of the herd. Ahead, a dark smear fading into the distance, showed the badlands—a maze of twisting cañons broken by eroding buttes and scattered high mesas, a far-reaching country where half the cattle in Colorado might have disappeared and stayed out of sight for days.

The slopes along the sides of the bowl-like depression were studded irregularly with cedar and scrub oak. Here they split, three men to a side, Luke and Steve Merritt and one of his men on the left, Flint and his two riders to the right.

They waited twenty minutes, until the herd was strung out along the depression below, before Luke brought the last drag rider into his sights and squeezed the trigger of his Winchester. It was his first experience at cold-bloodedly killing a man, but the nausea that gripped him gave way before a cool hatred as he recognized his target as Shorty Bates. Shorty's piercing scream was blended into the low hoof rumble of the herd. He sloped awkwardly out of the saddle as other guns took up the echo of that first shot.

Luke had counted eight riders. In the momentary lull following that first burst of gunfire, his swinging glance counted three men down. Then the margins of the herd bellied outward as the steers caught the quick panic that took the riders and he lost sight of the men below. Out of that writhing, bawling mass of cattle a gun started winking orange flame. A rider down there had been caught in the milling herd and was shooting to clear a way to safety. Abruptly three rifles on the slope drove in a hail of lead at him, and his shadowy form slid out of sight, and his gun abruptly ceased its hollow chant.

With the flashes of the guns on the slopes giving them targets, the riders below threw back a ragged, nervous fire. Luke picked out one of them and shot his horse from under him. Immediately someone below sent shot after shot at Luke's hiding place. He left the shelter of the tree and picked another, and for half a minute he levered shells into the magazine of his rifle, shooting coolly at the winking bursts of gun flame below.

Suddenly, in a lull that quieted all but one gun, Luke heard a sound behind him. He rolled to one side and looked back. Scarcely thirty feet away, a man stalked down the slope toward him, a gun in his fist. Luke's hand stabbed at his holster. He swung his Colt up and lined it as the man's .45 thundered. The bullet missed, and Luke's answering shot broke the man's run into a headlong, diving sprawl. Then, far to his left, another gun ripped away the sudden quiet. A blinding blow caught Luke on the side of the head and dimmed his senses. While he was struggling to overcome the slow paralysis that settled through him, he saw a shape loom over him and felt his weapon kicked out of his upraised hand.

He fought to clear his brain, yet for minutes his sight was dimmed and his hearing registered sounds feebly. He knew that someone had pulled him to his feet, that he was walking, but only when a blazing bright light burned through the lids of his closed eyes did he regain full control of his senses.

Directly ahead was a blazing fire, with men moving in and out of its circle of light. He felt a tight hold on his wrist and saw a man standing beside him. From out of the distance came the frantic bawl of the cattle blended with the rumbling of two thousand hoofs pounding the ground.

"They've headed 'em off," the man beside him said to another who stood across the fire.

Two men carried Steve Merritt up to the fire and laid him on a blanket. "He'll be out for a while," one of them announced. "I bent the barrel of my cutter over his skull."

Someone on the far side of the blaze sent out a quick challenge that was answered by a vaguely familiar sight. Two high shapes took on the forms of two riders over there, and a moment later Luke was staring unbelievingly at Sue Price, noticing that she was tied in her saddle. Beside her, swinging to the ground, was Bill Trench.

The Singletree ramrod strode into the light. "What's the count, Stalke?"

The man standing over Steve Merritt answered: "Shorty got it. So did Fencil and Curly. I don't know about the others. The boys are out quietin' the herd."

"The others? Storm and the rest?" Trench hadn't seen Luke.

"Storm's over there. Two of the others are dead. Flint McCauley's got a busted arm. They're bringin' him in."

Bill Trench looked across and saw Luke then, and came around the fire. He smiled mirthlessly: "So Shorty's lead poisonin' didn't work?"

"This jasper gut-shot Blazer," the man holding Luke announced. "You want me to take him out and plant a lead blossom in his scalp, boss?"

Trench shook his head. "Not yet. We'll keep him and the rest along with the girl . . . in case they've got friends who follow us." He was regarding Luke steadily. "I'll think up a good way to get rid of you when the time comes, Storm."

Then, before Luke understood his move, the ramrod brought his right fist up in a long, powerful swing. It caught Luke fully in the mouth. His knees buckled and his head fell drunkenly to one side.

Trench said: "Watch this jasper. He won't come to very soon, but, when he does, he'll make trouble. You'd better lace him up." He walked to the other side of the fire and spoke to Stalke. "We're campin' here until mornin'. Take the girl off her horse and watch her and the rest. You're in charge tonight. I'm taking Red and Jerry, and going back along the trail and see if anyone else is followin' our sign."

He mounted his gray and rode back into the shadows, toward the herd.

It was the pain in his shoulder that pulled Luke back to his senses. He shifted his weight quickly to his other side and lay there, breathing deeply while the throb of his wound subsided. His jaw hurt when he moved it. His lips were swollen and bleeding. He looked down over his feet and saw the fire thirty feet away. After his eyes had become accustomed to the light, he made out two figures squatting on their saddles near the warmth of the blaze and recognized Warren and Stalke. Each of them had a rifle between his knees.

Beyond them he made out Steve Merritt, lying with a blanket thrown over him. Sight of the blanket made Luke shiver, for he was out of the warmth of the blaze and his coat was gone and he was cold. He tried to move, but his wrists and feet were tied together.

Several other blanketed figures lay close in to the fire, but he couldn't recognize them. He was looking for Sue Price but couldn't see her. For minutes he lay there vainly trying to figure a reason for her presence here, and feeling a dull hopelessness at the turn of events that had so quickly changed things tonight. An hour—two hours ago—he and Steve and Flint had been sure of the outcome, but now. . . .

He heard a sound to one side of him, a muted whisper. He shifted his body and turned his head to look, studying the

131

vague shadows in the darkness. Then he saw Andy Mills's boy, crouching behind a scrubby bush not ten feet away. The youngster intercepted his look and nodded. His small face was pale. He was shaking from the cold, but his presence there could mean only one thing.

Luke looked across at the guards. Warren was lighting a cigarette, and, as Luke watched, he flicked the stub of the match into the fire. Stalke was dozing, his chin on his chest. Luke looked over his shoulder again, but didn't see the boy. Abruptly he felt something stir at his back, and then the kid was working at the ropes about his wrists. Finally he felt the ropes slacken. He moved his hands, ridding them of their numbness, and felt the cold touch of a gun barrel beneath his hand. He looked around and saw that the boy had left him and was once more hidden behind the bush.

Luke's lean fingers closed about the familiar handle of a Colt. He slowly sat up, making no sound. Now he could see Sue, and she was watching him from directly opposite with an unbelieving stare. He reached down and had already untied the knot at his ankles before Warren turned and saw him.

As the man's hand went to his rifle, Luke lined his six-gun on the man's chest. "Don't move," he said quietly.

Warren froze, with his hands half raised. Then Stalke woke and turned, and in his surprise he knocked his rifle to one side so that it fell to the ground. Both of them raised their hands.

"Where's Trench?" Luke queried, keeping his voice low.

Warren smiled wickedly. "Wouldn't you like to know?"

Luke thumbed back the hammer of his weapon, its *click* audible in the still air. "I want to know where Bill Trench is!"

Warren's color faded and he made an effort to swallow and couldn't. Then, as Luke rocked the gun barrel a bare inch, the man broke. "Don't, Luke! He's up on the rim with a couple others, watchin' the back trail."

The man's raised voice woke the others. Luke stood up, stepped back out of the light, and said: "One move out of any of you and I let you have it." He flashed a glance to his side, where the boy still crouched behind the bush. "Bob, go across and take those ropes off Sue."

The kid moved around the outside of the circle, approaching Sue from behind, sensing that to cross between Luke and any of the others was to invite a bullet in his back. In half a minute Sue was getting unsteadily to her feet.

"Untie Steve and any of the rest that are left." Luke's tone was clipped, hard.

A minute later Steve Merritt and one of his men were already on their feet when a gun crashed from above on the slope.

Luke felt the air whip of a bullet fan his face. He threw himself backward, behind the shelter of a low-growing cedar. Stalke made a stab at his rifle and was swinging it around at Steve Merritt when Luke threw his first shot to knock the killer forward on his face.

Merritt threw himself on a man who was rising out of his blankets and tore an upswinging weapon from the man's hand and brought it down solidly alongside his head. Then he ran over to help Flint McCauley to his feet. Flint's right arm was bandaged and he was weak from loss of blood.

From somewhere above a gun was sending its hollow thunder out across the draw. One of Steve's men grunted audibly and clutched his stomach and went to his knees. Luke saw Sue run back out of the light, dragging the boy with her, and then he was looking upward, seeing the shadowy bulk of a man outlined forty yards away and above. He took careful aim, squeezed the trigger, and saw the man pitch forward to the ground in a sliding roll that sent up a fog of powdery snow.

Another gun beat out up there, then another. Luke saw Steve Merritt get up and swing around in time to catch Warren lining a rifle at him. Both men fired at the same instant. Warren went down, and Steve stayed on his feet, running back out of the light.

Luke took one more shot at a Singletree rider crawling off into the shadows, and missed. Then he worked back from the shelter of the cedar to another higher up the slope. One of the guns up the hill began throwing a steady fire into the tree Luke had a moment ago deserted. Safe for the moment, Luke climbed higher above the fire, trying to spot a target.

Then, from close beside him, a gruff voice said: "Who's that?"

Luke turned, and at the same time Bill Trench rose up from behind a bent, snow-drifted bush. Too late, Trench recognized him. Both of them swung their six-guns into line. Luke's fast two shots were one prolonged gun blast. As he arced up the weapon and threw it at Trench, he saw the muzzle of the ramrod's six-gun blossom into flame. A blow at his thigh knocked Luke's right leg from under him, and he stumbled and fell.

Expecting each moment to feel the smash of a slug in his chest, Luke waited there, powerless to move. All at once Bill Trench's right hand dropped to his side, and his weapon slid from his grasp. He staggered a few steps toward Luke and suddenly fell, stiff-legged, face down.

They lay there, ten feet apart. Once Trench raised his head, and tried to speak, but the words were choked back in a stifled rattle.

Ten minutes later Steve Merritt found them that way. Bill Trench had crawled back until his outstretched hand was within inches of his fallen six-gun. Steve picked it up, ignoring Trench as he walked over to where Luke lay with his leg doubled under him.

Steve worked quickly, ripping away the trouser leg, carefully moving Luke until the pain had eased off. After half a minute's inspection of the wound, Steve straightened.

"That bullet must have knocked your pins out from under you," he said. "It's a clean hole, probably a sprain along with it. You'll be all right."

"Where's Sue Price?"

"Down there somewhere. She was helpin' Flint wrap a bandage around his busted arm when I left. She wanted to come after you, but I wouldn't let her."

"How about Andy's kid?"

"He's down there, too. We got 'em all, Luke . . . all but the ones ridin' guard on the herd. They cut out and headed down into the breaks. I don't reckon we'll see 'em again."

From far below they heard Sue calling. Steve answered, and two minutes later she and the boy climbed the hill. When she saw Luke, she ran to him and knelt beside him and cried: "Steve, is he hurt?"

"Nothin' he won't get over."

Just then they all heard Bill Trench muttering something unintelligible from where he lay ten feet away.

"You'd better go over and help him, Sue," Luke said.

She hesitated for a moment, then looked down at Luke and nodded to the boy, and walked over to where Trench lay talking in an undertone.

As the boy started to follow her, Luke said: "You stay with me, Bob. I haven't had a chance to thank you for what you did."

But the youngster only half heard him. He was standing there, listening intently, as though trying to catch Trench's low-spoken words. Suddenly the voice died away, and Sue stood looking down at Trench for a second, and then turned and came back to Luke once more.

"Bill's gone," she said, laying an arm about the youngster's shoulder. She looked down at him. "What he wanted to tell me was about your father, Bob. He said that Andy Mills was innocent, that he and Shorty framed him because they thought he knew what they were doing."

The boy's eyes lighted with pride. Luke, looking up at the girl, caught her faint nod that sealed their secret. He saw something else in her eyes, too, something he read as a promise of happiness to come.

The Matched Pair

"The Matched Pair", as the author titled this story, was the last short fiction he would write. It was sold to *Adventure* magazine on March 8, 1956, and the author was paid $500.00 for it. The title was changed upon publication to "The Devil's Pardner" when it appeared in *Adventure* (8/56). In 1929, at the University of Illinois, Jon Glidden met Dorothy Steele, and they were married the next year. In many of his stories, Dorothy was the model for the Peter Dawson heroines. Out of the 127 short stories and short novels that Jon Glidden published, this story remains Dorothy's favorite. For its first appearance in book form, the author's original title has been restored while the text is based on his typescript.

I

He was one of five passengers to get down off the mid-morning local, a small, square-shouldered man of wiry build wearing a black four-button suit. Had it not been for his sun-darkened face and wide hat, he would have looked like a drummer, and a poor one. He stood apart from the others as they boarded the hotel dray. As soon as the team of big work horses had hauled the top-heavy rig away, he sauntered to the street end of the depot platform, packed and lighted his pipe, and stood staring down between the double rank of weathered buildings, faded carpetbag sitting alongside his worn but polished boots.

After all these years, after the high impatience that had gripped him these two days and nights of travel, Will Knight was strangely reluctant to set about the errand that had brought him here. Simmons, the telegraph operator, noticed him standing there and after several minutes gave way to a strong curiosity, coming out of the depot and across to him to ask: "Need some help, friend?"

Will Knight looked around, strongly startled, for his thoughts had been elsewhere. His thin face took on a good-natured smile and he answered somewhat sheepishly: "Looks like I do. It's been too long to remember. But I was trying to think where Doc Stiles lives."

"Pine Street. That first one down there by the feed lot. Turn right. His house is the brick one halfway up the block."

"Much obliged."

Will shook the tobacco from his pipe, picked up his bag, and took the cinder path down the street, thinking that Ledge was a pleasant-looking town, bigger than he had imagined it to be after his brief glimpse of it that wild and snowy December night some seventeen years ago. But, of course, any town was bound to grow over such a span of time.

He readily recognized the doctor's brick house, although the blue spruce centering the front yard was stately and tall where it had been little higher than his head on that other visit. A sign on the porch rail bore the legend:

Richard M. Stiles, M.D.

Walk Right In.

His closing of the hall door brought the sound of a chair scraping against the floor in a room beyond. Then, before he quite had the chance of recalling the look of the hallway, the door of the inner room swung open.

Doc Stiles had aged. His hair was white, his frame portly where before it had been fined-down, slim. He held the door wide, nodding civilly, saying: "Come in, come in."

Will set his bag down alongside the umbrella stand and entered the office, a high nervousness making him breathe deeply of the antiseptic-tainted air. Stiles, closing the door, asked a trifle pompously: "What can I do for you, my good man?"

Will turned and eyed him soberly. "You don't remember me?"

The medico shook his head. "There've been so many. Have I treated you before?"

"No. My wife."

"Oh." Stiles stepped across and eased down into the caboose chair behind his roll-top desk. "What was her name?"

"Knight. Julia Knight."

A strict reserve at once thinned the doctor's benign look. "So," he breathed. In a firmer, clearly unfriendly, tone he stated: "You've wasted your time coming here. And mine. You wasted your time writing the letters, sending the money. I told you that."

140

"You did." Will's expression was a humble one, and there was a faintly beseeching quality in the look of his blue eyes. "Doctor, all these years I've been thinkin' there might be something you forgot. If there is, I've got the right to know."

"You already know as much as I can tell you. Can't be of any help at all. Not any."

"She's still alive, isn't she? Along with the boy?"

Stiles's glance fell away, too quickly. He was about to speak when Will quietly insisted: "She is. And you must know how to put me on the track of finding her."

"Didn't I write you she'd left? That the boy was stillborn?"

"You did. Only you forgot I was outside in the hall and heard the baby cry."

That evasive quality once again tinged the medico's glance as he tried to meet Will's stare, bridling. "Don't try and pin me down on a thing like that, man. How can a doctor remember every one of say a couple of thousand youngsters he's helped bring into the world? All I know is that your son died."

The numbness of futility was settling through Will Knight, although that quality of uncertainty in the other's manner kept a faint hope alive in him as he stated: "Julia's my wife, Doctor. And the boy's my. . . ."

"You damn' cheap tinhorn sport!" Stiles suddenly flared, leaning forward in his chair, gripping its arms. "Can't you get it through your thick head that she wanted no part of you? Of the life you dragged her into, of the crooked money you used to buy her those frilly rags? Whose idea do you think it was that night, havin' the marshal arrest you and take you back to that town where you'd used those marked cards?"

"Julia's?" Will was deeply shocked, for he had never known.

"Hell, yes! Who else's?"

Julia had been half out of her mind with pain and desperation that night, Will bleakly remembered. She hadn't been herself at all, and, thinking back on it, all he could say now was: "I had it comin' to me, sure. I was a year in that jail. It changed me."

"No skunk ever changes," Stiles retorted acidly. "Not even a denatured one."

"This one did."

Will lifted his hands outward from his sides, looking down at them. He caught himself on the point of thrusting out those work-worn hands and showing Stiles the calluses, the broken nail on the left index finger. It was on the tip of his tongue to ask the man if those could be the hands of a cardsharp, but then his strong pride rebelled. It was pointless to tell Stiles now that for twelve years after he had left that jail he had worked hard and honestly at every job he could find. How he had first cooked for a logging outfit, then hired on with a trail crew far to the south that was driving a herd of longhorns into Arizona Territory. It wouldn't mean anything to the medico to know that he had ridden for other outfits, that he'd worked the night shift in a silver mine, and finally driven for a freighting outfit hauling out of Virginia City until he'd at last saved enough to homestead.

It was also pointless telling the man that he had several times put by enough to make the trip across here only to be discouraged by the return of his letters and the money he'd sent Stiles for Julia. Only his stubbornness, his feeling of guilt, and his faint hope of prodding the medico into remembering something that would help him were responsible for his being here now.

Doc Stiles just wasn't the sort of man you could talk to and make understand. That was very plain to Will just now, although he nonetheless said quietly, doggedly: "It's cost me dear to make this trip. I'd be beholden if you could tell me anything . . . anything at all about Julia . . . where she went from here . . . how long since you last heard of her."

"All I know is that your wife and boy are gone, Knight. That was a long time ago. How would I know where they wound up?"

"You just said the boy died."

The doctor's glance slid away once again. He reached up and scrubbed his forehead in strong irritation. "Which is a fact. You got me so damn' rattled I can't think."

"Where's the boy buried?" A roughness edged Will's tone.

"Out there at the north edge of town in the graveyard."

"Just where in the graveyard?"

"How would I know? Jim Hanks was coroner back then. He passed away eight or ten years ago." Stiles had lost his sureness and concluded somewhat lamely: "Back then the county didn't have any funds to spend on such things. Maybe the headboard's even gone by now."

"Who looks after the burying ground?"

"Nobody. Oh, once or twice a summer the ladies at the church go out and pull weeds and such. But there's no one in charge . . . no one to keep track of the graves."

Will tried not to show his annoyance at this obvious hedging as he soberly said: "Doc, I'm not the wild kid gambler that got Julia off the stage and brought her here to have her baby that night. I was twenty then. Now I'm thirty-seven. I haven't handled a deck of cards or even packed a gun since that night."

"Don't mean a thing to me either way," Stiles countered.

"Doesn't it mean anything to you that I'm a father trying to find his boy? And his wife? Leave it up to them whether or not they take me back."

"I tell you I can't help you." Acidly the medico added:

"Wouldn't even if I could."

"If I hadn't thought your word was good, I'd have been here years ago," Will insisted. Now for the first time he lost hold of his temper and dryly added: "You could've cooked up a better story than this."

Stiles stiffened in indignation one moment. The next he burst out: "Why, you confounded. . . ."

His face reddening in fury, he suddenly reached around to jerk open the kneehole drawer of his desk. Thrusting aside an untidy assortment of papers, letters, and pamphlets, he rummaged around at the back of the drawer, growling furiously: "Just let me lay hands on that. . . ."

"You needn't bother."

All Will's anger had left him. In its place was a sharp disappointment and a growing contempt for this man. He turned away to the hall door, opened it. Abruptly a thought prompted him to glance around. The doctor was glaring malevolently at him.

"I'm riding over to the county seat for a look at the records," he said tonelessly. "If the boy died, it's got to be written down in a book somewhere. And if anyone in this settlement can put me on Julia's track, I'll find her."

"Clear out! And don't come back!"

Will closed the office door behind him, picked up his bag, and let himself out onto the porch. The early October morning still held some of the night's chill. The air inside the house had been only comfortably warm, yet his forehead was damp. He wiped it with a palm, tilting his wide hat far back on his dark head. Going down the yard path, his thoughts were such a jumble that he made the conscious effort of trying to ignore them.

But presently, as he neared the main street, he did grasp the fact that he had caught Stiles in an out-and-out untruth.

He doubted that the man's being rattled and surprised accounted for the lie. So it naturally followed that Stiles was hiding something. What that something might be, Will could only surmise. The medico might know that the boy was still alive. Or he might know of Julia's whereabouts.

Will's thoughts began coming a little straighter, clearer now as his dying hope slowly revived. He had come all this way to find Julia. He would start looking for her.

Turning down the main street, he passed several cabins and frame houses, a barn and corral, when he came abreast a shack with its single window proclaiming: **EATS**. It occurred to him that he hadn't eaten a meal since last night. So he turned in off the walk, entered the restaurant, and took the stool nearest the window at the front end of the oilcloth-covered counter.

Yet, when the waiter came to stand opposite him, asking—"What'll it be, mister?"—he found that the thought of food held no relish for him whatsoever. So he ordered only a cup of coffee.

He was taking the first sip of the coffee, his glance idly roving the drab room, when he happened to notice a pair of matched horn-handled Colts and a shell belt lying on the back counter alongside a coffee grinder. The waiter, noticing him eyeing the weapons, left the stove at the rear and came toward him asking: "Want a bargain, mister?"

"A bargain?" Will frowned in puzzlement.

The man picked up the holsters and belt and laid them on the counter in front of Will. "Got these last night. From a jasper that'd had his pocket picked on the southbound. Looked a tough one to me. He was busted and needed cash to get home. So he brought old Windy Burgess, the conductor, along to back his story. I was sucker enough to give him a gold eagle for the pair."

145

"Looks like you got your money's worth." Will pulled one Colt from its holster. It was a .44, well oiled and in good condition. "Not a bad buy at ten dollars."

"Or at twenty-seven. Only what'll I do with 'em?"

Will shrugged. "Ask twenty. They're worth that."

"You can have 'em for what I give him. Ten."

Shaking his head, Will said: "Wouldn't have any use for them, thanks. But somebody'll be along and take them off your hands."

"Hope you're right."

The man placed the guns alongside the coffee grinder and went on back to his stove. Will, sipping his coffee once more, looked out onto the street trying to think of where he would go from here to start looking for Julia. The first thing to do, he supposed, was to go across to the county seat and try to find some trace in the records about the boy.

A figure hurried past along the walk. It was a full two seconds before Will, deep in thought, was jarred from his preoccupation by recognizing Doc Stiles. No sooner had his attention quickened than he was seeing the medico look furtively back over his shoulder in the direction from which he had come. As Stiles hurried on out of sight, Will was attaching strong significance to that backward look. Doc Stiles gave every appearance of a man setting out upon an errand and not wishing to be observed.

Will was no sooner convinced of this than he was asking himself if his call on the medico might not possibly be the reason for the man's hurried trip down the street. The hunch was strong, not to be ignored. Quickly Will lifted his bag to the counter and called to the restaurant man: "Mind if I leave this with you for a spell? Say an hour or two?"

The other nodded agreeably enough. "Just so's you remember where you left it."

Will thanked him, said—"Here's something for your trouble."—and laid a quarter on the counter before turning to the door.

Coming onto the walk, he looked along it to see Stiles already a hundred yards distant, still hurrying along at a far faster gait than became a man of his age and portly proportions. He stood a moment, hesitating. Then, the hunch still strong in him, he left the walk and cut obliquely over the street to its far side, hurrying as a four-team freight hitch bore down on him.

He went along the far walk keeping pace with Stiles as they reached the double rank of stores at the town's center. Twice more over the next half minute the doctor turned and peered back up the street again, as though wanting to be sure he wasn't being followed. He evidently saw nothing to cause him alarm, for he kept hurrying on without slackening stride.·

Directly beyond a saloon, Ed's Monte Parlor, Stiles abruptly left the walk to climb the verandah steps of a new two-story brick building. Will watched him disappear through the double doors, only afterward noticing the sign above the ornate entranceway: **RANGE PALACE, 1892.**

Will stopped short, for the moment at a loss as to what he should do next. He had nothing to go on, nothing at all to assure him that Stiles's visit to the hotel had been prompted by his talk with the medico earlier. Yet the tough-fibered, stubborn streak in him wouldn't let him overlook his hunch, having followed it this far. So he sauntered over into the nearest store's recessed doorway and leaned against the window corner, alertly eyeing the hotel verandah obliquely across the way.

He idly noticed a passing wagon headed upstreet, its scrawny team driven by a Sioux who wore his black hat flat-crowned and his shirt tails out. Across the way two youngsters, boys, were making a game of splashing each other at the hotel's iron watering trough. He saw a man and a woman come out of the hotel entrance and stand talking at the verandah rail. As the minutes dragged on, he had a hard time keeping a tight rein on his imagination and forcing himself to wait here rather than cross the street and follow Stiles into the building.

When the medico finally did reappear, Will almost missed seeing him. For Stiles came out of the narrow passageway separating the hotel from an adjoining store. He paused briefly at the head of the passageway and appeared to be carefully scanning the street in both directions. Then he turned down the walk, his stride now only a slow saunter, and in a few more seconds disappeared into a store several doors below.

For all of half a minute after the medico had gone from sight again, Will stood debating what he should do. An indefinable excitement deepened his breathing at the realization that Doc Stiles just now hadn't been in a hurry. He had obviously finished whatever errand had brought him here in such haste.

The fatalism so deeply imbedded in Will Knight's nature finally took him out and around the nearest tie rail, over the width of the street, and up the hotel verandah's steps. He hesitated just short of the double doors. Then, squaring his shoulders, he pulled one door wide and entered the lobby.

It was deserted except for a woman and a little girl sitting in chairs alongside one of the street-facing windows and the clerk behind a counter that ran between the stairway and a pair of closed double doors Will supposed must lead to the dining room. He hadn't thought out exactly how he would set about getting the information he was after. But, as he approached the counter and as the clerk glanced up at him, he found himself casually asking: "Is Julia around?"

"Julia?" Every muscle in Will tightened as the man nodded perfunctorily toward the pair of closed doors nearby. "Right in there. She ought to be settin' up the tables for dinner."

Will stood a brief moment in a complete paralysis of surprise, feeling the pound of his pulse at his temples. He cleared his throat of a sudden dryness. Turning then to the doors, he pushed one of them open and stepped into the dining room.

For a moment he thought the room was empty. Then all at once a jingle of silverware swung his attention to the far, shadowed corner. A slender, small woman in a blue dress was working at a table across there, her back toward him. Even before she turned her head to glance quizzically in his direction, her dark red hair told Will Knight that he had found Julia.

She straightened and slowly faced him. Although the light was bad, he plainly saw her freeze in sudden recognition. He could feel her hazel eyes warily measuring him, running the length of his slim frame. He instinctively reached up and took off his hat as he made his way slowly across between the chairs until only the width of a clean-clothed table separated them.

The years had dimmed Will's memory of the electric, heavy sensation he had so often experienced when courting Julia. It all came back to him now. He saw her as being fair and proud, her small-waisted figure still youthful-looking, still graceful of proportion. Her eyes held that same quick intelligence as of old. The eyes rid her freckled face of its plainness. They could be merry and mischievous, he remembered, holding an invitation for the man who could see it, or for the man she would let see it.

She was much the same, only now she was a mature and attractive woman. None of that merriment shone in her eyes this moment, yet he oddly remembered it as a blend of excitement and remorse stirred in him. Now he realized as never before how much his foolishness and his headstrong ways had cost him.

When she didn't speak, but only stood staring at him wide-eyed and almost afraid, he blurted out: "I'd give my right arm, both arms, to live it over again, Julia. The part that had nothing to do with you and me."

Her bewildered expression thinned and died. A faint smile touched her lips, although it wasn't mirrored in her eyes. "Your arms, you say? But what about your hands, Will?"

Her face was pale, and her words held the bitterness of gall. He understood their meaning all too clearly and gently answered: "The hands don't count any more. Except for handlin' a horse. Or a rope or harness and such."

She took this in with a barely perceptible nod, seeming to accept it as truth. Her cheeks had gradually taken on color, and abruptly her face was as he remembered it, gentle of expression, radiant and vital. For an instant it seemed that something he had said had pleased her, although, when she spoke, her tone didn't match the softness shining in her eyes.

"Doctor Stiles was here a minute ago. He told me he'd seen you."

"I know. I followed him here. The old fool wouldn't give me a thing to go on."

Julia smiled faintly, seeming little surprised and hardly interested in his explanation as she told him: "He couldn't. He knew he'd be hurting too many people if he did."

"I still say he took a lot on himself."

"Did he?" She eyed him speculatively, almost aloofly. "Will, I've been happy. Until now. Why did you come back?"

"Because. . . ." For an awkward moment he was at a loss for a way of expressing himself. Then he lamely answered:

"Maybe it's because I'm different from what I was. I want you to think better of me."

"Are you so different?"

Once again he detected that strong bitterness in her, and he thought: *It doesn't become her, but it's my fault.* It was on impulse that he tried to reassure her by saying: "I'm not staying, so you needn't worry. You have your own life, and I don't mean to horn in. If there's another man, that doesn't count, either. But I had to know. About you. And about the boy. All these years I've wanted to know. Only Stiles sent back my letters."

It seemed that a shadow settled across her face, although the light shining through the verandah windows hadn't dimmed. "Yes, the boy," she breathed softly. Then her head tilted higher and she said in a firmer voice: "There isn't another man, never has been." Over a pause, and in faint embarrassment, she went on: "I can see the change in you. I'm glad for it. What are you . . . where are you living?"

"Way off west in Wyoming Territory. Near the mountains, not far from a town. A good town. Raisin' horses for the stages and the freight outfits. It's good range. I'm making it better."

"Then you've given up. . . ."

"The cards? Gave them up that night eighteen years ago." He took in the wondering light in her eyes and soberly nodded. "That other's like something I dreamed and hate lookin' back on. You might say I come of age that night here in Ledge. Then and over the next year, before they turned me loose."

Her look was troubled, and she could no longer meet his steady regard. "I'm sorry for that, Will. I was sorry the next day, but it was too late."

"We can be glad it happened before something rougher

did." He was remembering her look of some moments ago and asked: "But what of the boy? Stiles got his tongue twisted enough to let me know the baby didn't pass away that night."

"No." Her glance met his once more, her eyes bright with an anger that made him wonder what he had said to offend her. "He's alive. He's big and fine and . . . he's in trouble."

Will's thankfulness at learning he had a son was short-lived. "Trouble? You mean real trouble?"

"Yes. Real trouble."

"Can you tell me about it?"

"I can. But it wouldn't help."

"Tell me anyway."

Julia sighed gently. "I've had to piece it together from what I've heard, from what people have told me. For you see, Will, no one knows he's mine. No one."

"How have you managed that?"

"Think back. I didn't want the baby. Not then. Now I'd give. . . ." She briefly closed her eyes, as though to dispel some aching regret. "Late that night the doctor was called to a house in town to deliver another baby. The woman was alone. She lost her child. So I . . . Doc Stiles came home toward morning. He looked in at my room to see if I was resting. When he found me awake, he told me about it . . . about not having had the gumption to tell the woman what happened to her baby."

After a brief pause, she went on: "He was going back to wake a neighbor and get her to look after the woman, to get her to tell what had happened to the baby. I . . . I made him give her our boy, Will. She's never known but what he was her own."

Will felt a stir of strong indignation from deep inside him. But then that emotion drained slowly away as he thought back upon the circumstances of that December night so long ago. He was to blame for what Julia had done. The cards were to blame.

So he only nodded, saying: "Maybe I understand. Anyway, it was your right."

"It wasn't. But I didn't realize that till it was too late. So I did the next best thing . . . stayed here close to my boy to make sure they treated him right. No one has ever known. The woman and her husband are fine, God-fearing people. They moved out onto a ranch when George was three. They've given him a fine raising. He's so serious and . . . well, thoughtful and nice."

"His name's George? George what?"

"Meeker." Julia laughed uneasily, but happily. "He's got my hair, Will. Only lighter, a real carrot top. And he's a good head taller than you."

He smiled in response to her attempt at relaxing the tension between them. "Good for him. Takes after my old man. Didn't I tell you once I wanted no runts like me in the family?"

The softness that touched her glance that instant hurt him, made him yearn to take her in his arms, and he quickly changed the subject. "This trouble you mention. What is it?"

"Cards." She regretted the bluntness of the word the moment she uttered it, for she saw Will wince. She hurried to say: "It's not what you think. He isn't fond of cards. He only comes to town once a week and it's natural for him to want to be with his friends and his father's crew. I don't think he touches drink."

"Shouldn't. He isn't old enough."

Julia nodded, explaining: "Last Saturday night he was watching a game of draw at Ed Moore's place next door. He had the bad luck to see one of Ed's dealers cheating. Caught him at it and called him on it."

When she hesitated, Will asked tonelessly: "Then what?"

"This gambler has a reputation with a gun. It's known he killed a man over in Cottonwood a year ago." She lifted her shoulders in a meager shrug. "You can guess the rest. George wasn't carrying a gun, never does. When Shoup called him a liar, George went at him with his fists. Some men pulled them apart. But Shoup had the last word. He's threatened that they'll meet again the next time George shows up in town. And he's told George to be carrying a gun."

"George isn't backing down?"

Julia shook her head. "No. The talk is that he'll be here today, the same as always. The Meekers come to town once a week and usually eat their noon meal here in the dining room every Saturday."

"Can't his father put a stop to this?"

"He's not that kind. He knows his boy is in the right and he won't see him back down to such a thing."

Will tried not to notice the moistness that now brightened the look of Julia's hazel eyes. "The boy could keep clear of this cardsharp till things have cooled off."

"He could, but he won't. There's . . . forgive me for saying it, Will, but there's too much of you in him. He won't back down to a thing like. . . ."

Behind Will there sounded the *creak* of door hinges. He looked around to see the counter clerk standing in the doorway just as the man said: "Julia, the boss'd like to see you upstairs in the office. Right away."

"Tell him I'll be right along." Julia waited until the door had swung shut before saying: "There's nothing can be done to stop this, Will. Nothing. All I can hope for is that my prayers will be answered."

A cold anger roughening his tone, Will asked: "Isn't there

some kind of law around here that can stop this?"

"Law?" Julia laughed mockingly. "Jim Hood's our law, our marshal. He couldn't stop a fight between . . . between two school kids."

Wearily, resignedly, Will shook his head. "Then all we can do is hope."

"That's all." Julia tried to smile, couldn't. "Well, I have to go now. Mister Blake doesn't like to be kept waiting."

"Do I get to see you again, Julia?"

She regarded him steadily a long moment, then abruptly shook her head. "No. I'd rather you didn't. It's too . . . it wouldn't help either of us. This has been hard enough."

A sharp disappointment struck through him, and he told her: "On the way across here on the train I got to dreamin', Julia. Got to wonderin' if. . . ." Hesitating, at a loss for words, he tried to make a fresh start. "This place of mine's got a snug cabin on it. Two rooms, with water piped in from a spring. A creek runs right through the meadow. This time of year the quaking aspen turns the side of the mountain so bright with orange it fair blinds a man. It's a choice spot." He felt his face flushing as he went on, speaking quickly now. "Julia, I'm only thirty-seven . . . with a good half my string left to play out if luck holds, with a lot of good years ahead of me. You're only thirty-four. I just want you to know that the place is half yours if. . . ."

"No, Will! Don't say it!" Her voice had taken on a high pitch of real alarm. "I've been too long forgetting how it was with us. I . . . it could never be right between us again. Not ever."

There were tears in her eyes, and suddenly she came from behind the table, stepped quickly past him, and hurried to the door.

The sound of the latch clicking held a finality for Will

Knight that was unarguable, that told him positively he'd seen the last of Julia.

With a slow, tired sigh, he made for the door. Beyond it, he crossed the lobby without looking at the clerk, who was eyeing him quizzically. He was glad when the lobby door swung shut behind him and he stood in the bright sunlight at the foot of the verandah steps once more.

II

He turned aimlessly down the street after leaving the hotel, his thoughts wholly absorbed in looking back on those few short minutes with Julia. He had failed miserably in convincing her he was a changed man. The scar he had put upon her seventeen years ago was too deep to be forgotten. He had lost her the night George was born, lost her irretrievably, and now he was feeling that loss more deeply than ever before.

He came to a street intersection, crossed to the opposite walk, and started back the way he had come. As he drew opposite the hotel, he eyed it longingly, vainly trying to think of a way of changing Julia's mind about him. Then, completely at a loss for an idea, his glance shuttled idly on along the far walk to take in the slow traffic of customers going in and out through the swing doors of Ed's Monte Parlor.

Thinking back on what Julia had said of George Meeker's run-in with Shoup, the saloon gambler, he was all at once consumed by a strong curiosity to lay eyes on the man. Before he had quite defined the impulse prompting this curiosity, he was leaving the walk and stepping out around a buckboard, his boots lifting puffs of dust from the hoof-churned margin of the street.

An abstemious man, Will had only upon rare occasion visited a saloon since that other visit to Ledge so many years ago. Now, as he turned off the walk, pushed aside the swing doors, and entered this one, the smell of the tobacco and whiskey-tainted air brought back a flood of unwanted memories that only heightened his sense of loss at Julia's refusal of a few minutes ago. The wide room was lit by shaded coal-oil lamps hanging over the long bar and the half dozen gambling lay-outs opposite. Because this was Saturday, there were already upward of twenty customers in the place even though the clock above the bar mirror proclaimed the hour to be ten minutes short of eleven. Most of the customers were standing at the bar, but others sat at two of the poker lay-outs, four men at one, five at the second.

When the apron came to take his order, Will asked for whiskey. As the man set a stoneware bottle and a glass in front of him, Will remarked: "How's Shoup's game going?"

The other shrugged. "This one's for low stakes. A game never hots up till late in the afternoon." As he spoke, he glanced in the direction of the rearmost of the two poker lay-outs.

"Hear he's got himself primed for a meetin' on the street this afternoon."

The saloon man regarded Will more closely a moment. What he saw evidently satisfied him, for he drawled: "Yeah. We tried to talk the damn' fool out of monkeying around with a kid. But he's got the bit in his teeth, thinks he was put upon. So it's his affair."

"This George Meeker's pretty well thought of here-abouts?"

"George? Hell, yes." With a worried shake of the head, the apron added: "Could be George'll come through it with no more than a scratch. Or a busted arm or such. I'm one that's hopin' so."

He moved away to wait on another customer. Will, as he poured himself a scant finger of whiskey in the glass, glanced back to the rear poker lay-out. Shoup was easily recognizable as a house man. The other four players were plainly range-bred, their faces dark from the sun, all four wearing hats. Shoup was bare-headed, his black, wavy hair shiny with pomade and neatly combed. He wore a black vest over a dark maroon shirt, the sleeves of which were held up by garters. He was smoking a cheroot, one eye half closed against the tobacco's lazy curl of smoke. He was young, probably in his early thirties. His vest hung open and bulged at the left side over a shoulder holster, the strap of which was in plain sight crossing his flat chest.

A slow rise of anger gripped Will Knight as he tried to size up the man and couldn't. Shoup was either a dangerous man, or he was making good the bluff of being one so far as these townspeople were concerned.

Disgust strong in him, Will looked away, called to the apron, paid for his unfinished drink, and went out onto the street again. His glimpse of Shoup had only heightened his worry over George. He felt impotent, inadequate in dealing with this situation. He could do absolutely nothing to help his son.

He took out his watch and was about to glance at it when he remembered having noticed the time by the saloon clock. On the train this morning the conductor had told him that a northbound ran through Ledge at two o'clock each afternoon. Now, as he went back up the street, leaving the stores behind him, he remembered having left his possibles at the eat shack out near the depot and decided he would eat the noon meal, go on up to the depot, and wait there to take the two o'clock and begin the long trip back home.

This part of his life was finished. In the coming months he would try and erase from his mind all thought of Julia, of George. They had their lives to live, their problems; he had his own. Julia had clearly shown him that he wasn't to interfere.

The restaurant owner seemed glad to see him, greeted him cordially. There were two other customers sitting at the front, so Will took a stool halfway back along the counter and ordered a meal. As a plate of stew was set before him, he was doing the same thing he had earlier, absent-mindedly eyeing the pair of .44s in their holsters on the back counter alongside the coffee grinder.

"They're still for sale, neighbor. And at the same price."

Will stirred from his preoccupation long enough to look up at the man, smile wryly, and say: "Not for me."

He began his meal, forcing himself to eat. Try as he would not to look back over the past hour, Julia's image kept shuttling before his mind's eye. He could clearly remember the proud tilt of her head, the softness of her glance, the several unguarded moments when she had seemed to show something like a real affection for him. Yet all that counted for nothing now. He had lost her as surely today as he had that night here in Ledge so long ago.

Thinking back across his life, and looking ahead upon the life he was returning to, Will Knight saw little to please him. He faced only the bleak prospect of living the rest of his days alone, a solitary man sharing nothing with anyone, even though throughout the years he had worked hard in the hope of one day finding Julia and proving to her that he had in him the makings of a good and honest man. With that hope gone, nothing mattered any longer.

He no longer cared about himself, or about what happened next. Building up the ranch and his horse herd had lost all meaning. The cabin and the lush-grassed meadow became in his mind's eye just another lonely spot among the hills, no different from a hundred others. His life was as good as over except for the dreary years ahead, with middle age, and finally old age, creeping relentlessly upon him.

It was at this point in his bitter reasoning that Will Knight thought again of his son, and of what was to happen to George today. With a sudden and knifing dread he knew that he might not be taking the two o'clock train north, for he would have to stay here in town long enough to know what happened to George Meeker in his meeting with Shoup, the gambler.

That sobering thought made him abruptly aware of his surroundings once again. He found himself sitting with fork in hand, his half-finished meal completely forgotten. The two other customers had paid for their meals and left without his having been aware of it. Unconsciously, he discovered, he had once more been staring fixedly at the pair of horn-handled revolvers on the back counter directly opposite him. They served just now to remind him that George would probably be carrying a similar weapon today, perhaps within the hour, when he came to town for his meeting with Shoup. Will wondered just how familiar his son was with the use of a handgun and, wondering, thought back on how he himself had carried one almost every waking moment throughout those few early years when he had been a gambler.

He had been a passable shot, although he had never been called on to use a gun against a man. Nonetheless, he had faced that prospect without the slightest qualm and strangely without ever having given really serious thought to being hurt, or even killed, by a better man than he. Back then, he supposed he'd had either too much courage or too little sense to care a great deal what happened to him.

George, from what Julia had said, was of a different breed than he had been. So was he himself a different breed these days. Were he in George's place today, he judged he would care a great deal what happened to him.

"But would I?"

No sooner had he startled himself by whispering those words aloud than he knew the answer without any doubt whatsoever. After what had happened this morning, he wouldn't care, not in the slightest. So now he stared at the pair of .44s with a new and acute awareness. Very deliberately, thinking it through, he made up his mind to something that gave his thin and hawkish face a wary, alert expression.

Quite suddenly he was ravenously hungry. He began eating once more and presently was scraping the last of the gravy from his plate and licking his knife. Laying the knife back on the plate, he wiped his mouth with bent forefinger, and glanced back to where the restaurant man was working at the stove.

He straightened, saying with a casualness that belied the faint excitement stirring in him: "Say, I've been thinkin' it over. About those irons. If you're still of a mind to let them go for ten, I'll take 'em off your hands."

The other looked around, his face at once taking on a pleased smile. "Fine, neighbor. You get a bargain, I get my money back."

He came along his counter, picked up the guns, and set them down in front of Will, who had laid a gold eagle and a silver dollar on the oilcloth. "Want your grip?" the restaurant man asked and, when Will nodded, went on up to the front of the room to lift the carpetbag from the floor.

Will took the bag, opened it, and dropped the guns and the heavy belt inside, buckling it shut again. He took his change from the man, said—"Good meal."—and let himself out the door.

He turned down the walk toward the center of town and had taken but half a dozen strides when he abruptly halted, eyeing the open gate of the small, slab-fenced yard alongside the restaurant shack. He stepped over and peered through the gate to find half the yard's width grown rank with weeds, the half adjoining the shack piled high with split, neatly stacked cordwood. A chopping block with an axe imbedded in its top stood amid a litter of chips on the near side of the wood stack.

Will glanced both ways along the walk to find it empty. He went on in through the gate then and across to the fence end of the stack of cordwood. He opened the carpetbag, took out the guns, then pushed the bag deeply into a hole between several rounds of wood and the fence before straightening to pull his coat aside and swing the heavy shell belt and holsters about his waist.

The weight of the guns had no sooner settled against his hip bones than he was remembering a long-forgotten feeling. The holsters hung snugly, their ends at fingertip level just below the bottom line of his coat. False though it was, the feel of the heavy guns against his thighs gave him a sense of completeness, of sureness. He drew first one of the .44s, then the other, rocking open the loading gates and spinning each cylinder to find it loaded except for an empty chamber under the hammer. Whoever had worn these guns had known how to carry them safely.

Letting the coat hang open, he drew in a slow, deep breath, and expelled it, for the moment wondering if he was setting out upon a dangerously foolhardy errand. In the end he couldn't and didn't particularly care. Shrugging the thought aside with a finality that was absolute, he stepped toward the gate.

III

The crowd inside Ed's Monte Parlor had grown during the past hour. Over half the men lining the bar's length were here out of curiosity alone, having heard of George Meeker's run-in a week ago with Ed Moore's gambler. More than a few were friends of the Meekers, and they stood about doing little drinking, gathered together in small groups, their talk low-pitched, serious. Others, for the most part townsmen whose habit it was to hang out in such places as this, were openly betting on the outcome of the impending meeting, giving heavy odds in Shoup's favor.

The clock above the bar showed fourteen minutes short of the noon hour when one of the men watching the play at the front faro lay-out noticed a small, black-suited individual wearing a wide hat pushing his way in through the batwing doors from the street. The man elbowed his neighbor, saying in a low voice: "Who's the banty packin' all the hardware, Jim?"

His companion followed his glance, whistled softly in surprise at sight of the twin holsters showing beneath the newcomer's coat. "Stranger to me. Looks like a rough one, eh?"

Will Knight, having stepped clear of the doors, was aware of the furtive glances being directed at him. It had been the same coming down the street, for it was an uncommon thing these days to find anyone, even a law officer, wearing a pair of guns. Ordinarily Will would have been ill at ease knowing himself to be the center of attention. Yet just now he was like a man standing apart from himself and coolly observing what was happening to someone else. He scarcely gave the matter any thought as he moved from behind a pair of men blocking his view of the back poker lay-out.

His nerves came taut as his glance went back there. Shoup sat in the same chair, shiny black hair gleaming in the lamp-light. Will sauntered back along the bar, then in between two crowded tables until he stood behind the man sitting opposite the gambler. It was a full minute before the five players at the lay-out finished the hand, one of the five swearing soundly as Shoup laid down the winning cards.

Shoup was smiling faintly, reaching out to pull in the assortment of varicolored chips at the table's center, when his glance happened to lift, shuttle slowly around the room, then come to rest briefly on Will. He saw Will soberly eyeing him, and his glance fell lazily away. But then his eyes came wider again as he took in the twin holsters showing beneath the line of Will's coat. For the barest fraction of a second his hands went motionless before sweeping in the chips.

That hesitation in the gambler told Will that the man was very aware of him. Now Will stepped around to the only vacant chair at the table, one twice removed from Shoup. He pulled the chair back, asking: "Room for one more?"

The player to his right, sitting alongside Shoup, looked up and nodded affably. He was telling Will—"Your money's good as . . ."—when the gambler cut him short by quickly inserting: "Game's about over, stranger. Wouldn't be worth your while."

On the way down the street a minute ago, Will had emptied his purse in his pocket. Now he reached for the pocket, asking tonelessly: "You're a house man?"

At Shoup's answering nod, he laid three double eagles on the green felt, knowing that, if he lost them, he wouldn't have enough money left to buy his ticket home. He eased down into the chair drawling: "Then let's have the deal."

The quiet arrogance of the act made Shoup's jaw muscles tighten until they stood out against the sallow hollowness of his cheeks, and Will was aware that moment of the bulge of the shoulder holster beneath the man's vest. This was an awkward, tense moment that Will pretended to ignore completely. Two of the men sitting opposite frowned uneasily, one of them quickly inserting: "Leave him buy in if he wants. Hell, we might be here another hour."

Shoup finally lifted his sloping shoulders in a grudging shrug, counted Will some chips, and pushed them across, picking up only one of the three double eagles. "It's a bit early in the day for that kind of money," he dryly stated. "Lose those and you can buy more."

"Suits me."

It was as the man to Shoup's right was picking up the deck and shuffling it that Will spoke again, asking in apparent innocence: "How come the game's folding?"

"Shoup here's meetin' a gent out front any minute now. For what you might call a friendly get together," answered the man who sat between Will and the gambler.

"Any reason why the rest of us can't keep on when he leaves?" Will wanted to know.

"There is, stranger," the other answered enigmatically. "But suppose you wait and find out what the reason is."

The deal was made. Will picked up a pair of niners. No one raised Shoup's opening bet. On the draw Will was dealt a third nine. Shoup bet again. Will raised, and the man opposite raised again. The gambler raised still a third time. Will called, and the man opposite grumbled unhappily and tossed in his hand. Shoup laid down two pair, Will showed three nines and gathered in his winnings.

"Good way to begin," the gambler stated impassively as he picked up the cards and shuffled, but his gray eyes wore a chill look as he glanced briefly at Will.

From then on Will watched the man's slender-fingered

and supple hands. Shoup handled the cards with superb ease, as well in fact as Will had ever seen anyone handle a deck. As the cards were cut, then finally dealt, Will had to admit that the gambler's fingers moved too fast for his unpracticed eye to follow and be positive that no wrong move had been made.

Will picked up his hand to find that he held three queens. He had barely glanced at the cards when there came an interruption. A man had come across from the bar, and now leaned down close behind Shoup to say quietly but plainly audibly: "Meeker and his old man just pulled in. They're eatin' next door."

Shoup nodded perfunctorily, dryly observing—"Plenty of time."—as he picked up his hand and glanced at his cards.

They went on with the play, Will not improving his hand on the draw. He placed his bet; the man alongside him raised; Shoup raised. Will, after a moment's deliberation, folded his hand and tossed it to the table's center, whereupon the gambler commented agreeably enough—"No guts, eh?"—and matched the remaining player's raise.

Shoup took that hand with a seven high straight against the other's three kings. As the house man was gathering in his winnings, Will couldn't begin to guess whether that hand had been based on luck alone or on Shoup's skill with the cards, but he knew what he had to do, regardless. He didn't even take cards on the draw the next hand, which was dealt by the player to his right. There was little action on the hand, which was won by one of the players sitting opposite Will.

When he reached out to gather up the discards and take the deck, Will could feel his hands trembling momentarily. But then, as he began the shuffle, a calm settled over him. The first two times he shuffled, his hands felt stiff and clumsy. But then his fingers seemed to limber up as he moved them faster, as he saw Shoup carefully watching him.

That strict attention the gambler was giving him was what Will had been waiting for. He began the deal, went all the way around. The second time around he slipped Shoup the deck's bottom card. He saw the house man straighten slightly. The next time around he dealt even faster, but fairly. But the fourth time he once again slipped the bottom card out and tossed it to Shoup.

The card had barely left his fingers when Shoup reached out and with a vicious down swing of the fist pinned his left hand, the hand keeping the deck on the table.

"Hold it!" the gambler called loudly. He glanced briefly at the others before adding: "Boys, we've got a sharper among us! I saw it. Twice I saw it! The bottom card."

Will slowly pulled his hand from under Shoup's. He put his palms on the table, sensing that the sound of voices and laughter had died out in the immediate vicinity of the table, that the man between him and Shoup had pushed his chair far back. Now was the instant he'd been waiting for.

Suddenly he leaned forward, reached out and with a hard, full swing of his left hand, struck the gambler squarely across the face. The next instant he lunged halfway up out of his chair, bent at the waist, both hands lifted slightly outward from his sides at elbow level, fingers clawed.

"Tinhorn, you've just ordered yourself a head stone. You're a liar!" Will let those quiet-spoken words carry their weight before asking: "Anyone else see what he says I did?"

He kept his gaze riveted on Shoup's flushed face as one of the men opposite answered: "Not me." Then the player to Will's right put in: "Me neither. Calm down, Shoup. You been seein' things."

The house man had sat rigidly through this interchange. But those last words prodded him to a higher pitch of fury, and he burst out: "Twice I saw him do it. To me! He's crooked, I tell. . . ."

Will's left hand slashed out again to cut him short. The hand caught him fully on the side of the face, tilted his head hard around. As his right hand lifted instinctively toward the holster beneath his vest, Will also moved, his right hand slashing back, swiftly brushing coat aside and settling to the handle of the .44.

Shoup froze. His eyes came wider open in a sudden, panicked realization that he was in serious trouble. Very slowly, very carefully, he laid his right hand on the green felt.

"Go ahead, try for it," Will said tauntingly.

The gambler's Adam's apple bobbed as he attempted to swallow, couldn't. He shook his head, and naked fear was showing in his eyes as Will told him: "Then get on your feet and head for the street."

"No." That one word was all Shoup could summon.

Will stood slowly erect. He gave the man a disdainful, belittling regard as he reached across with left hand and took his double eagle from the stack of coins in front of the gambler. Then, in the driest of tones, he drawled: "You were meeting someone out there on the street, they said. Well, sir, I'll be right out there waiting for you. Only I get first try at puttin' a hole through your yellow hide!"

He pocketed his money, and backed slowly out from the table. Men made way behind him, gave him a clear path to the aisle running between bar and gaming tables. He didn't turn his back on Shoup until several men blocked his view of the gambler, who was on his feet now and protesting loudly, helplessly.

Turning, Will headed deliberately for the doors. Every muscle in him was tight, every sense alert for the slightest hint of something that would signal danger behind him. Yet as he made the doors, he could still hear Shoup's voice raised in outrage, and that alone told him he was safe.

He came onto the walk, letting his breath go in a gusty sigh of relief. As he left the walk's edge and stepped down into the street's dust, he was looking back and thinking over the past minute, satisfied at its outcome. Perhaps, if his luck held, he had it in him to help George, after all.

IV

In the hotel dining room, George Meeker all at once laid his napkin alongside his nearly full plate of food. "Can't eat all this stuff, Pa. Why am I sittin' here waitin'? Why don't I get it over with?"

"Suit yourself, Son. I just didn't want you rushing into this."

"Then I'll be at it." George, a tall and gangling young man with brick red hair and a serious, round face, pushed his chair back from the table, breathing: "Thank the good Lord you made Ma stay at home."

The elder Meeker nodded impassively, betraying not an iota of the emotion seething in him. He was fond of his boy and wouldn't let himself think of what might be happening out there presently. His voice was gruff as he said: "You've got my blessing."

"You're not comin'?" George was on his feet now.

"Not just yet. You're on your own. I'll tag along in half a minute and watch." As an afterthought, the older man added: "Just you wait for him out front. Make him come to you."

"He'll come. He's primed."

"Best shed your coat and throw it over the porch rail. And remember. You never hit nothin', bear nor hawk nor deer, without aimin' at it. So take your time and get his middle across your sights before you pull."

"I'll remember, Pa."

"And damn the man that's afraid of anything! Don't be of this four-flusher."

"You know I ain't scared."

"Then God go with you. You're in the right, George."

171

Julia, who had some moments ago happened to look through the kitchen door's glass inset and saw George rising from the table, watched her son turn and walk toward the lobby. Her heart was thumping as she understood that the moment she had been dreading had finally arrived.

She quickly pulled off her apron, tossed it onto the china table alongside the door, and called to the cook: "Ed, I'm feeling faint! Think I'll go outside for a breath of air."

"Take your time, Julia. Me and Maud can handle things."

Julia smoothed back her hair, opened the door, and crossed the dining room to the lobby. Coming onto the verandah, she was trying to appear unconcerned as she saw George directly ahead of her slowly going down the steps to the walk. He had shed his coat. She could see the handle of a gun wedged between his belt and dark brown shirt.

Sight of the weapon numbed her, filled her with stark apprehension as she came to stand at the verandah rail and looked out across the street. Of the half a hundred figures she could see on the nearby walks and moving back and forth across the street, that of a small, white-shirted man wearing a pair of guns and standing obliquely across the way momentarily caught her eye and held it.

The man was leaning indolently against the end gate of a wagon, his arms folded across chest, his coat thrown over the wagon's near side board. Perhaps it was the oddity of seeing anyone wearing twin holsters that made her examine him with a fleeting interest, then look away. It was only after her glance had swung beyond him toward the saloon awning directly below that she sensed something familiar about him, and looked at him again.

She caught her breath sharply as she recognized him. "Will!" she cried, barely audibly. "What are you doing here?"

Will Knight had barely glimpsed the man he took to be his

son, recognizing him by the color of his hair, when he saw Julia come out onto the hotel verandah. Sight of her brought a second hard shock, this one a blend of pleasure and deep concern. As that emotion was rising in him, the last of his doubts was gone. He was humbly grateful for the quirk of fate that had brought him here. His only regret was that, no matter which way this went, Julia would be hurt.

His very attention swung once more to the opposite walk, to the door of Ed's Monte Parlor. Instantly he saw that the appearance of the red-headed man had caused a stir of interest across there, for several men who had been loafing in front of the saloon were now moving in through the doors, obviously carrying the word to Shoup.

Above the saloon other onlookers were clearing the walk, edging toward the shelter of store doorways, nearly all of them looking downstreet in George Meeker's direction. Surprised that so many of these townspeople should have been forewarned of what was to come, Will glanced back over his shoulder to find this near walk's edge lined almost solidly with still more people, those closest eyeing him with an open curiosity tinged with respect.

He understood two things, then: first, that there had been a lot of talk about George's meeting with Shoup; next, that word of his own run-in with the gambler had traveled fast. He could feel the tension that lay along the street now. Hardly a man, and only a few women, were moving along the walks as George Meeker paced slowly out around the hotel's iron watering trough toward the center of the rutted and dusty thoroughfare.

For a fleeting moment he studied George. What he would make out of the boy's features lifted a strong pride in him. George appeared older than his years, his face showing a seriousness and a maturity, and he stood tall and erect, his tanned and freckled face bespeaking long acquaintance with the outdoors. His rangy frame had a work-hardened look. There was no softness about him, and for an instant Will Knight looked back across the years and was stabbed by a keen regret that he hadn't been George's kind in his youth. Had he been, things might have turned out far differently.

Suddenly a hush settled along the street. The dying away of the voices of those people on the walk behind him made Will glance quickly toward the saloon. He was in time to see the swing doors moving outward before Shoup's spare shape.

In another moment the gambler stood alone on the empty walk across there. He came to the walk's edge, looking squarely across the street's width at Will who had eased out a pace from the wagon's end gate. Now Will heard a scuffling of boots against the walk planks behind him and knew that people were hastily moving out of line with him and Shoup.

Will thought—*Now's what counts.*—an instant before the gambler called truculently across to him: "You, over there! Keep out of this."

Will let a long moment's silence bear on the man before quietly answering: "No. Count me in."

"The hell I do!" There was a bluster, a false bravado to the words. "You stay clear till I've. . . ."

"Shoup! Here I am!"

George Meeker's deep-toned voice cut the gambler short. He was too far away to have heard this interchange between Shoup and Will, and now he spoke a second time, calling: "Move out. Get clear of the walk."

Shoup glanced quickly in George's direction, but then looked warily back to Will. Some of the bluster had gone out of him now. He opened his mouth to call something when George once more cut him short. "Come on, man! Either get out there or I come after you."

Will hadn't moved a muscle, didn't intend to until it was necessary, knowing that his presence alone was roughing the gambler's nerves. Even with what George had just said, Shoup still hesitated under the threat of Will's two guns.

George Meeker could have had no inkling at all of what was wrong with Shoup, for all at once he was impatiently striding toward the man. The gambler swung halfway around to face him, vest hanging loosely over the holster high on the left side of his chest.

When George was but half a dozen strides short of him, Shoup lifted his right hand a spare inch upward along his side. But then that arm went rigid, motionless, as he saw Will's small shape tense and buckle slightly at the waist.

George was coming in on the empty tie rail directly beyond the gambler when all at once Shoup made a final, desperate attempt at evening the odds against him by crying out: "Damn you both! How's a man going to take on the two of you?"

A puzzled look crossed George Meeker's face. Will saw it plainly as his son halted, having rounded the end of the tie rail. "What fool nonsense you talkin'?" George wanted to know. Then, not giving Shoup the time to answer, he started for the man again, growling: "Pull that thing and use it if you're not afraid!"

He was within a stride of the walk's edge when the gambler took one backward step. The look on Shoup's sallow face was one of panic as he seemed suddenly to realize that he couldn't run his bluff, couldn't bull this through even with the false courage he'd managed to muster over several drinks at the saloon's bar.

At the last moment, as George stepped up onto the planks in front of him, Shoup tried to save himself by bellowing: "Now wait! Give a man a. . . ."

George's lunge, and the driving smash of his fist, cut the gambler's words short. Shoup tried to dodge aside. But that vicious and unexpected jab caught him hard at the base of the neck and spun him halfway around.

He made the mistake then of reaching toward his holster. George's left hand slashed out, caught his wrist, twisted it down and around. The gambler groaned in agony as the arm was lifted in behind his back. He screamed as the arm suddenly gave way.

George hit him once more, threw a driving uppercut that caught him on the jaw hinge. He had fainted dead away even before his knees buckled and he fell face down on the planks. He wasn't even vaguely aware of George, rolling him onto his back, jerking his gun free of the holster, and throwing the weapon far out across the street.

Shoup's short-barreled Colt skidded into the dust barely two feet outward from Will's boots. He stared down at it, then across the street where a noisy, boisterous crowd was gathering about George and the gambler's prostrate form.

Men were running across the street to join the crowd as Will stood a moment looking toward the hotel. The verandah was empty except for a lone man who stood watching the commotion on the street below. Will was never to know that this was George Meeker's father. Julia was gone.

Will turned and reached for his coat, pulled it on. He made his unobtrusive way to the walk and turned up it, the sudden realization that George was safe, that his worry was over, making his knees feel rubbery and weak. He was trembling all over. But for the moment he was as happy as at any time he could remember.

V

It was a lazy, bright afternoon, with only a touch of autumn's chill in the air. Will sat on one of the benches on the depot's sunny side. He was enjoying his pipe, pulling slowly on it as he absent-mindedly listened to the click of the telegrapher's key sounding through the open window of the depot office close by.

Off in the distance he heard the moan of a train's whistle. He took out his watch. It was thirteen minutes after two o'clock. As trains ran their schedules these days, the two o'clock was right on time.

He looked down at his carpetbag, noticing the bulge the twin holsters made. He smiled sparely but in genuine delight as he thought back over George's meeting with Shoup. He would remember it always, recall its every detail. He would hang this matched pair of Colts on the wall of his cabin to help him remember.

Once again the train's whistle shuttled in over the town, this time out of the near distance. Will straightened, reached down to knock the dottle of tobacco from his pipe. He heard quick steps sounding against the platform planks and knew he no longer had the place to himself. When the sound of those steps abruptly broke off, he glanced incuriously around.

Julia stood there, not twenty feet away.

Stiffening, Will took in her tight-waisted coat and small blue hat trimmed with a verbena-like flower. Her left hand gripped the handle of a varnished straw suitcase.

Will's pulse was pounding at his temples as he came hastily erect and reached up to take off his hat. For several seconds he stood staring at her, unable to find his voice. He hadn't for an instant hoped he was ever to see her again.

"Will, I . . . I heard after it was all over what you did."

He nodded for no particular reason, saying awkwardly: "Wasn't much, Julia. More luck than anything, the way it turned out."

"It wasn't luck. George will hear about it and wonder."

"Let him wonder."

"Yes, let him." Seriously she told him: "Doc Stiles set Shoup's shoulder. Then the marshal told him he had to leave and not come back, ever. So he bought a ticket on the next stage. The marshal saw him leave."

"Fine. Then George's trouble is over."

"It is, Will."

Ill at ease, he asked: "You're taking the train?"

Julia's only immediate answer was a hesitant smile. Then she came slowly toward him, as though wanting a better look at his face, at his eyes. For she was peering at him intently as she unexpectedly asked: "You meant what you said? About . . . about your place being half mine?"

A tightness gripped Will Knight's throat. A surge of pure ecstasy lifted in him then as he went to her, gathered her in his arms.

He gave her his answer as he drew her very, very close.

Phantom Raiders

This story was completed in early October and submitted by Jon Glidden's agent to editor M. Goodman at the Red Circle pulp magazines on October 28, 1938. It was apparently misplaced in the editorial shake-up that followed at Newsstand, publisher of the Red Circle magazines, because it was Fred O. Erisman, M. Goodman's replacement as editor, who bought the story two years later, on October 10, 1940, paying the author $70.70. Jon Glidden's title for the story was "Phantom Raiders of Bull Forks". This was changed to "When Blood and Guns Brand a Man's Backtrail" when the story appeared in *Western Novel and Short Stories* (2/41). For its first book appearance, the author's original title has been somewhat shortened.

I

Neil Harper took five weeks to work his way the three hundred miles from Malpais south to Bull Forks. Anyone interested enough to follow him would have been curious to find that he took his time, that he apparently had no pressing business on hand, and that he invariably brought trouble with him. Yet, nothing about him invited any such curiosity, and therefore there was none. He stood an inch under six feet, not very tall according to the standards of a range where tall men were the rule rather than the exception. His outfit was inconspicuous, Levi's, a brown flannel shirt, and gray vest—and often, on chill days, a canvas Windbreaker. His wide-brimmed Stetson was gray, comfortably limp and soiled, and his boots were worn and never polished. The Colt .38 that rode at his thigh had a scarred walnut handle and the holster was plain. Packing a gun was a precaution most men used in this country. His eyes were a pale blue and his face was lean and bronzed and his straw-blond hair was bleached. He had the look and easy manner of a common cowpuncher.

The day after he was last seen in Malpais, the safe at the Esmerelda Mine was blown open and robbed of thirty thousand in gold bullion. While he was in Ledge, a herd of six hundred and forty prime shorthorns vanished across the peaks of the Sentinels, and in the end the sheriff's posse knew only that four riders had made the drive. The night before he sloped down into Prairie City a freight was derailed, the train crew bound and gagged, and sixty-four choice cow ponies unloaded from the cars and driven off into the night. The horse herd was well below the border five days later, and once again a sheriff returned empty-handed and carrying the news that

181

this was the work of the same four outlaws.

Middle Arizona ranchers sent their second complaint of the last three months to the Cattleman's Association, demanding that a crew of range detectives be sent in. The ranchers had good reason, for a late fall spread of the sleeping sickness had killed off a big share of their saddle stock and the loss of that fresh horse herd meant a cattle roundup dragging out a month longer than it should have. These last outbreaks of lawlessness were on top of others that had started as long ago as early April.

Putting up at the Bull Forks Hotel his first night in town, Neil Harper's casual mention of having just ridden in from Prairie City made him the unwilling center of a curious group of serious-minded men. They were mostly Bull Forks merchants, but a few were ranch owners. These last put their questions intently, wanting particulars on how the outlaws worked, whether or not they'd ever been seen. "Just so we'll know what to expect when they start in on us," one of the ranchers said ominously. It was obvious that every man in the group expected Bull Forks to have its share of bad luck before long.

Neil Harper didn't have much to tell them. While he was doing his best to answer the questions, he was relieved to see a familiar figure cross the hotel lobby and join the outer fringe of the group. This man had a hawkish, dark face, a square jaw, and his heavy-built frame outfitted with a little more care than was a man's habit in this country. He wore a dark brown suit that showed signs of having recently been pressed, his shirt looked freshly laundered, and the black cigar he smoked was obviously a good one.

Neil nodded across to him and said: "There's a man that can maybe tell you more about it. He was in Prairie City last week when it happened."

The stranger smiled agreeably and took the cigar from his mouth, announcing: "The name's Porter, gentlemen, Phineas T. Porter of Tucson. I'm here to buy cattle." He paused long enough to puff once at his cigar, timing the gesture so as to let their attention settle on him. "Yes, I was in Prairie City and saw the sheriff and. . . ."

At this point Neil Harper walked quietly away from the group unnoticed. He climbed the stairs. He stood for ten minutes on the top landing listening to the drone of voices from below. He could see all of the group, but he watched Phineas T. Porter particularly. Finally his blue eyes narrowed at a thing one of the men said. It was: "Hell, none of us can tell when they'll start things poppin' down here! Take that payroll comin' from the east by stage tomorrow. Ten thousand, isn't it? Then there's the bank with that cracker box of a vault. We ought to make George Hoops tear out that thing and buy a new one. They might even take a likin' to my critters, or yours, Abe. . . ."

That was all Neil Harper waited to hear. He went to his room and turned in. As he lay under the blankets, a smile was on his lean face. Once he mused, half aloud: "A stage with a ten thousand dollar payroll in the boot! And a cracker box vault in the bank. Not bad." His last conscious thought before sleep crept in on him was that he would have to be awake at three in the morning.

He was awake at three. At seven minutes past the hour he was quietly going in through the small door at the front of the livery barn. He paused in the darkness up front only long enough to hear the hostler snoring on his cot in the small office. He passed the stall where his roan was stabled and at the saddle rack he took his rawhide reata from his saddle. He went out back and into the corral where a dozen ponies were kept. He carefully unwired the pole gate and pushed it open. It took the horses several minutes to stray out of the enclosure. Neil roped the last one to drift through the gate.

He fashioned a halter out of his rope, and astride the livery gelding he choused the small horse herd two miles out into the open country beyond town. At the first gray light of the false dawn, a half hour later, he was in the fenced pasture of a ranch four miles east of Bull Forks, riding down a rangy black horse. He roped it and led it outside the fence, leaving the top two strands of the wire sagging and making an opening which a horse would have had no trouble jumping. Then, putting the halter on the black, he turned the livery gelding loose, even drove him a mile or so back toward town.

An hour after sunup he was buying a worn-out McClellan saddle and a horsehair bridle from an old Mexican at an adobe house close in to the trail that ran east between Bull Forks and Flint City. The Mexican also fed him a breakfast of fried eggs, chili, and tortillas. It was while he was sitting in the shade of the adobe's narrow *portal,* finishing his after-breakfast smoke, that he spotted the four riders far out along the trail toward Bull Forks. As though this was a signal he had been awaiting, he swung onto the black horse and struck east again. In ten minutes of steady going he had left the four riders out of sight behind.

He caught sight of the stage shortly before eight o'clock. It was two miles out along the rolling sweep of grama grass range, laying a slow-settling boil of dust behind. Neil reined the black around and rode back half a mile to the steep shoulder of a deep arroyo where the trail dipped abruptly downward to cross a dry streambed.

Ed Medford, the stage driver, knew each twisting and rut of the trail, and it was therefore natural that he should swear as he slowed his two teams and kicked home the brake ten yards short of the sharp down pitch into the arroyo bottom.

"Grab onto somethin'," he told Bill Moss, the new man riding shotgun alongside him. "All I can ever do when we hit this spot is to hope the damn' rig won't tip over. Why the hell don't the county put in a bridge?"

Medford was intent on managing the teams, and Bill Moss had hung his shotgun on the rack below his knees and was holding with both hands to a seat brace as the stage tilted and lurched down the sloping bank of the wash. When the loud explosion of a shot cut loose, the top-heavy vehicle was swaying so badly that Moss couldn't trust himself to let go with his hands and reach for the Greener.

Ed Medford shot a glance up the wash and saw a blue cloud of powder smoke drifting away from the face of a waist-high rotten sandstone outcropping. The crown of a gray Stetson showed above the outcropping, and the sun glinted brightly from the sight of a six-gun. Medford dropped the reins and lifted both hands as the stage rocked to a stop along the bottom of the wash.

Bill Moss hesitated, even let his left hand edge down below the level of the seat. But that gesture brought a second explosion from the gun behind the outcropping and Moss's wide-brimmed felt hat was knocked off his head by the bullet. His hands jumped to the level of his ears.

"Throw down what's in the boot!" Neil Harper called, lowering the tone of his voice and making it as gruff-sounding as he could.

The driver obeyed instantly, keeping his hands in plain sight as he reached down and lifted from the boot a small but heavy metal-bound box. He dropped it into the sand beyond the front wheel at the exact instant the stage door swung open.

A tall, gray-mustached man stepped down out of the stage. He turned and spoke sharply to a girl who started to follow him: "Stay where you are, Betty!" Then, whipping his glance up to the driver, he intoned flatly: "That's a month's payroll for half the outfits on Bull Forks' range, mine included. Are you goin' to sit there and let him get away with this?"

The girl called in alarm—"Please, Dad! You might be hurt!"—but was silenced by a stern look from her parent.

Ed Medford lifted his whip out of the socket, lowered his hands to grab the reins. "There ain't nothin' we can do, Mister Graham," he said respectfully. He knew old Henry Graham well enough now to feel a real apprehension for fear the salty rancher would draw the six-gun he always wore in a shoulder holster under his coat. "Better climb in and let him have it. I'm gettin' out of here right now!"

Henry Graham was a stubborn but not a foolish man. When Ed Medford's whip swung back and then out, the rancher reached up to the hand rail, and, when the teams lunged into the harness, the rancher swung up onto the step and edged through the door. The teams slogged up the far slope and out of the draw.

Three minutes later, as the Concord rocked over the uneven trail, the muted, distant blast of a gun sounded out from behind. Ed Medford stopped the teams, said caustically to Bill Moss: "There goes the lock on the money chest."

Henry Graham opened the door and stepped down into the dust, looking back toward the broken line of the arroyo's gash. Medford looked off that way, too, and a few seconds later they both saw a rider on a black horse appear where the trail climbed out of the wash.

Medford said dryly: "Bill, if you'd brought a Winchester instead of that damn' blunderbuss, I might knock him off from here." The distance was nearly half a mile, but Medford had a great faith in his abilities as a marksman.

The guard remained silent. From below, Henry Graham said gruffly: "He's circlin'. Get along, Medford. The bank ought to know about this right away."

Medford pushed his teams hard for the next five miles. He and Moss watched the rider on the black swing gradually back into the trail and then draw out of sight ahead. On the long pull up the grade where the trail made a bend around the high shoulder of Squaw Butte, Medford looped the reins over his arm and filled his cob pipe. "That's the first time I've been held up in five years, Bill," he said. He added hopefully: "Like as not it'll be another five before anyone tries it again."

The Concord was drawing even with the high-piled rock mass of the butte's near low shoulder. Three seconds after Medford spoke the brittle *crack* of a rifle sounded above the creak of the harness and the ring of the iron tires. The bullet whistled past Bill Moss's face so that he snatched the reins and tugged at them viciously, bringing the lead team raring back on their haunches.

Two masked riders sloped down into the trail ahead of the stage. Another pair, wearing bandannas over their faces, appeared beyond the end of the rotten rock shoulder and fell in behind. Each rider had a pair of six-guns in his hands.

Henry Graham shouted up from the stage's front window: "Now what's wrong? Medford, I said to. . . ." His voice broke off abruptly as he saw the riders.

The tallest of the pair ahead reined in alongside the front wheel on Medford's side. "Empty the boot, driver!" he snapped.

Medford answered without lowering his hands. "There's nothin' but mail sacks to throw down, stranger. Another gent helped himself to the payroll five miles back."

The gray eyes above the bandanna covering the outlaw's face hardened. "Climb down," he ordered. He turned and motioned with a six-gun to Henry Graham. "Pile out, both of you!"

When Medford and Moss were standing alongside the coach with their two passengers, the tall outlaw said to his partner—"Watch 'em, Curly."—and swung quickly out of the saddle to climb up onto the driver's seat. He rummaged through the contents of the boot, then crawled back along the top and went through a valise and a small trunk in the rear rack, leaving Henry Graham's clean shirts and extra trousers strewn across the varnished top of the stage along with Betty Graham's dresses. "Nothin' here!" he called down to the others.

Abruptly one of the pair behind let out a muttered oath and called: "Driver, what did he look like? The jasper that got the payroll."

Medford shook his head. "We didn't get a look at him. But he forked a black horse."

The man on top climbed down off the driver's seat. A slow burst of anger was settling through him. Not ten minutes ago he and the rest had stopped a stranger on a black horse as he rode up the trail. They had asked about the stage, and the stranger had pointed it out, approaching in the distance. He now remembered the bulging bandanna that had been tied to the stranger's saddle horn. He'd had ten thousand in currency within reach of his hand and hadn't known it.

If he hadn't been seeing red, he might have reached down with his six-gun and clubbed Henry Graham over the head instead of shooting him. As it was, the rancher had waited for his chance and thought he saw it. The three other riders had drawn away a little and were talking in low tones, not looking at him. With his back to the man on the driver's seat, Henry

188

Graham thought he could hide the motion of his hand as it jabbed in under his coat toward his holstered weapon.

But the outlaw above saw that furtive move. He rocked a six-gun into line, thumbed a blasting shot, and Henry Graham staggered and fell back against the side of the coach as his daughter screamed and ran over to him.

As the girl knelt beside her father, the man who had shot the rancher stepped across to his horse and swung into the saddle. With a curt nod to his three partners, he rammed his spurs to his bay horse and led the way at a hard run down the trail.

A little later one of the four said: "He's gone."

They had ridden hard since leaving the stage behind. Yet here, with a vast westward spread of range stretching out before them, they could see no rider down the long line of the trail.

Spud, the one who had shot Graham, said: "You'll have to hand it to him. He's slick, stoppin' to talk to us the way he did."

Mel Dewey, the fattest of the four, laughed softly. "And I was goin' to ask him what he had in that bandanna slung from his saddle." He shook his head and added more soberly: "This is goin' to make the boss good and sore."

II

Neil Harper was sitting on the porch of the hotel when the stage came down the street shortly after one o'clock. He sauntered down and joined the crowd that formed around the stage, worried to see that four men carried one of the passengers, the gray-haired oldster who had wanted to fight this morning, to a doctor's office across the street. He saw, too, that the girl in the blue dress followed the wounded man.

He listened intently as Ed Medford told the story to the crowd. "Then, out by Squaw Butte, four more stops us. All wearin' masks. They was plenty riled when they found someone had beat 'em to it. Graham made the mistake of goin' for his cutter. One of these jaspers was up on top goin' through the express and saw him do it and cut down on him."

Bill Moss put in: "Caught him in the left shoulder, in the back. We're hopin' it missed his lung. He bled like a stuck pig. Take a look at the floor in there and see for yourself."

Back in his chair on the hotel porch once more, Neil Harper wondered idly if he had forgotten anything. He had been back in town by noon and he was fairly sure no one had seen him walking the quarter mile down the steep hill that backed the street to the south. He had unsaddled the black horse in a shallow coulée beyond the hill, turning the animal loose and knowing that before night he would have worked his way back to his home pasture. Along the lip of a narrow coulée behind the hill in back of the street he had found a sandy cutbank and caved it in on the saddle and the ten fat bundles of paper money he had taken from the stage's money chest.

It was while he sat at the first seat along the lunch counter

190

in the restaurant two doors below the hotel a quarter of a hour later that Neil Harper saw the heavy-built rider walk his horse down the street. There was no mistaking the scar along the sorrel horse. This man was one of the four he had met along the trail near Squaw Butte this morning.

He left his piece of apple pie half finished at the counter, paid for his meal, and went out onto the walk. The sorrel horse was at the hitch rail in front of the hotel, the rider climbing the steps. Neil crossed the dusty street and leaned against an awning post in front of the harness shop, taking his time about building a smoke.

His cigarette was half smoked when he saw the rider come down the steps and saunter along the walk to turn in at the swing doors of the nearest saloon. Neil was about to cross to the hotel when a second man turned in at the hotel steps, a spare-framed oldster on whose vest was pinned a five-pointed star that caught and brightly reflected the sun glare. Neil stayed where he was.

The sheriff was in the hotel for only five minutes. Once he reappeared, he walked along the street to the jail in a hurried, choppy stride and went into his office. As Neil crossed the street to the hotel, he felt the impulse to break from his slow saunter and hurry, but he ignored that inner warning and any men watching him would have decided that he was one of the habitual town loafers.

As he was about to reach out to pull open the screen door to the lobby, someone inside pushed it outward. Phineas T. Porter stood in the opening. He saw who it was, smiled broadly in an expression that didn't fit his narrow, chiseled face, and said: "Just the man I'm looking for." He gestured with a hand toward the chairs that sat along the rail. "There's something I wanted to talk over with you, stranger."

Although that same inner wariness was cautioning Neil

191

Harper to hurry on up to his room, he followed Porter over to the rail and sat in a chair beside him. Porter's look abruptly changed to one of soberness. "I didn't want anyone to hear us," he said in a low voice. "But the sheriff was just in at the desk asking questions about you. Something about digging up a saddle beyond the hill back here. He claims someone saw you walkin' down there around noon."

Neil smiled thinly. "Maybe they've got a law here that says a man can't go beyond the town limits."

Porter shrugged his shoulders. "I thought you ought to know. These tank town lawmen don't have much to do but be curious. And today the sheriff's got his mind on this stage robbery and is noticin' anything out of the ordinary."

"Thanks," Neil said as he stood up. "I'd better gather up my razor and make myself scarce. After holdin' up the stage this mornin', I halfway had my eye on that vault over in the bank as a good way to pass the evenin'." His thin smile belied the words.

Porter laughed. "Not a bad thought if you're short on change."

Passing the desk in the lobby, Neil noticed that the clerk eyed him sharply. He gathered up his belongings in his room and put them in the saddlebag he took from beneath his bed. He left a dollar and a half on the granite-topped washstand and went down the back stairway and into the alley behind the building. He crossed the street to the feed barn a hundred yards from the hotel. Five minutes later he paid the hostler his feed bill, and climbed into his saddle and rode out of town.

Three miles east of Bull Forks he came to a bridge and put the roan into the stream below it and followed it for two miles south, into the shallow folds of a low range of hills. He left the stream along a wide rock shelf and by three in the afternoon had circled to a point a mile to the west of town. Well hidden behind a towering cottonwood, he found the roofless ruin of a small one-room adobe house. There was a growth of sparse grass close by.

As he took the bit from the roan's mouth, he said: "How'd you like to try robbin' a bank with me tonight, Specks?"

Mel Dewey rode in at the camp, five miles to the north of Bull Forks, at dusk that evening. He swung his ponderous bulk from the saddle in front of the cedar fire, loosened the cinch, and asked Curly, the man on the rear side of the blaze: "Where do I stake him out?"

Curly jerked a thumb in the direction of a low knoll dotted by a stunted growth of cedars. "Back there," he said.

Spud Siringo was hunkered down across the fire and watching Tim Donegan mix the dough for the pan bread. He called: "Mel, stay here! Curly, take care of his jughead." When Curly had walked out of sight into the shadows, leading Mel's sorrel, Spud asked: "What's shapin' up in town?"

Mel said: "Plenty! Our lanky friend that got away with the payroll was in town. Only he cleared out in time to make a fool of the sheriff."

Spud stiffened. "Go on," he drawled.

"Seems a gent saw him walkin' down that hill to the south of town around noon. The sheriff heard about it, couldn't get it through his head why a saddle bum should like to walk so well. So he climbed the hill and had a look. He found an old Army hull buried under a caved-in cutbank up there and some sign leadin' to the place from the east. He came back to the hotel and found the clerk hadn't seen the stranger all mornin'. That got him to thinkin', so he went back to his office and went through his reward notices and ran into one that had the stranger's picture on it." Mel paused to take a drag at his cigarette.

"What did the dodger say?" Spud asked.

"He's wanted for murder, holdin' up a train, bank robbery, and cattle stealin'." Mel grinned broadly. "Looks like we've got some competition, eh?"

"Who told you all this?"

"The boss. He said to forget this stranger and get to work on this bank job, tonight if we can swing it."

Spud scowled down at the fire. "Why can't we wait a few days?"

"The sheriff and a couple dozen others picked up the stranger's sign and are followin' it. If they don't catch up with him today, they're campin' out overnight."

Spud smiled thinly. "So the town's empty."

Mel nodded. "It ought to be easy. Give me six-inch length of balin' wire and I'll have the lock to that back bank door open in two minutes. A tomato can full of giant powder will blow the front off the vault. We can finish the job in ten minutes."

Spud was thinking of something else. "They'll probably be thinkin' the stranger's one of our crew, won't they?"

"That's the talk the boss is givin' around," Mel answered. "This stranger was in Prairie City about the time we ran those bronc's off. Here's another thing. The boss don't think this gent is leavin' yet. He says to keep our eyes open for him."

A smile lacking all mirth took possession of Spud Siringo's gaunt face. "We'll know what to do if we do meet up with him," he drawled.

Mel shook his head. "The boss don't want him dead. He's hid that payroll, and, until we know where it is, he's worth a damn' sight more alive than he is buried."

"You mean we're to let him alone?"

"We're to let the boss know right away if we run onto him."

Tim Donegan was once more busy at the fire. "The boss usually has things figured right," he ventured to comment.

But Spud's look was still one of sultry belligerence. Mel and Donegan could read his thoughts. Once or twice Spud hadn't agreed with the boss; they both knew that it was only a matter of time until it came to a showdown between the two. They were now reserving judgment and neither of them much cared who bossed them in the end.

Spud said irritably: "Shake a leg, Tim. We'll move out of here as soon as we're fed."

"One thing more," Mel said to Spud. "The boss gave me hell about shootin' that old jasper this mornin'. That was Henry Graham, owner of the G Bar. He's worth more money than any man in this country and he was one of the men the boss came here to do business with. He says you've nearly spoiled his chances."

"What did he want me to do, sit there and let this Graham cut down on us?" Spud growled.

Mel shrugged. "He didn't say. But the old gent may have a hard time pullin' through. The boss is goin' to call on his daughter this evenin'."

Spud had nothing further to say. They ate their meal in silence and rode away from the camp half an hour later. As they picked up the winking lights of Bull Forks in the darkness ahead, Spud said curtly: "Tim, you'll stay with the horses in the alley. Mel and me will work the vault. Curly will take the front windows and watch the street. All we're bringin' away is coin and paper money."

They rode on in silence, coming in along the flat open country directly behind the north side of the street. They sloped out of their saddles in the deep shadow of a woodshed two doors below the bank's rear entrance. Mel didn't have to be told what to do. He took a piece of wire from his pocket, pried into the door's keyhole, and after a moment drew out the wire and bent it into shape. Ten seconds later the bolt of the lock eased back, and he pushed the door wide open.

He and Spud and Curly silently entered, Curly going along the counter to the plate-glass doors at the front. Shades were drawn at the door; Curly pulled one of them back a bare two inches and stood looking out on the street. Spud and Mel went to the vault. Spud carried a foot-long length of fuse and a tomato can full of black powder in one hand, a bulging saddlebag of dirt in the other. "We'll need some water to set this clay," he told Mel in a low voice. "See if there's a fire bucket handy."

Tim Donegan, under the eaves of the woodshed in the alley and holding the reins of the four ponies, couldn't help but feel a little nervous. It was late but not too late for the street to have quieted down. He listened to the sounds from out there, trying to identify them and staring along the passageway that led to the street directly across the alley from the woodshed.

If he had been looking down the alley, he might have made out a man's moving shadow that crossed the narrow lane beyond the bank. A minute later, if he had ignored the sounds from the street and concentrated on the nervous lifting of Mel's sorrel's head, he might not have been quite so taken by surprise.

All the warning he had was the barely audible scrape of a boot behind him. He wheeled, glimpsed a man's tall shape in the deeper shadow behind. A split second later, as his hand instinctively dropped toward his holster, the hard stroke of a six-gun barrel alongside his head knocked him into unconsciousness.

Neil Harper caught the reins of the four ponies as Tim Donegan sprawled on the ground. He tied the reins to a loose board in the siding of the woodshed, then dragged the outlaw back out of sight, close to the foot of the wall. A quarter minute later, at the exact instant the earthy pound of the exploding giant powder cut loose from inside, he was hugging the brick wall of the bank to one side of the open rear door. His Colt .38 was in his hand.

There was a long ten-second silence. Then someone on the street shouted hoarsely. A man's heavy boot tread sounded on the board floor immediately inside the door of the bank. Curly stepped out the door. Spud's voice inside grated curtly: "Hurry it up, Mel!" Spud came out to stand alongside Curly. He held a heavy moneybag in his left hand, his right fist was clenched around the handle of the six-gun still in the holster at his thigh. Mel came out a moment later.

Neil let Mel get clear of the door. Then, as they stood grouped almost within reach of him, he drawled flatly: "Reach, gents!"

Spud whirled, drawing as he moved. But as he faced Neil's rock-steady six-gun, his hold on his weapon went loose and the heavy .45 fell back into leather. Mel bent forward at the waist, tense, as though thinking of making a try at this tall stranger. But in one hand he clenched the necks of two small heavy money sacks and in the other arm he held tightly to his chest several bundles of paper money. In the end he had brains enough not to move his hand toward his gun and invite a bullet through his thick middle.

"You can dump it right there," Neil drawled. He heard a man running toward the alley along the passageway on the far side of the bank behind them, and added: "It's goin' to crowd you to get away."

Spud rasped: "You go to hell, you. . . . "

197

His words were choked off by the blasting explosion of Neil Harper's six-gun. An instant ago Neil had seen a man run into the alley out of the passageway. He had swung his weapon in a narrow arc and thumbed his shot. The man sprawled back out of sight, and Neil heard him running back along the passageway, calling something to others who must have been standing on the walk along the street.

Spud and Mel and Curly had their backs to the passageway. They hadn't seen the man and didn't know that the shot was intended for him, not them. The lead had whistled past Mel's left shoulder and made him suddenly let go of the money sacks and the bundles of currency. He said: "Easy, stranger! You can have it!"

Spud was held a brief moment in impotent rage, but Mel's giving in finally decided him. He dropped the one money sack he was holding. "We'll meet up with you one of these days, stranger," he said. "And when we do. . . ."

"Any day," Neil cut in. "You'll find me about three tomorrow afternoon in that busted-down house a mile west of town . . . in case you're interested. We might get together on a few things. There's some of this I can't handle alone."

Abruptly a gun far up along the alley spoke in two staccato explosions. One of the bullets hit the bank's brick wall and ricocheted in a high whine from a point barely a foot above Curly's head. He turned and ran toward the horses. Mel and Spud followed a second or two later.

Before they were out of sight in the darkness, Neil picked up the money sacks and the bundles of bills and was running back along the alley. He hugged the deep shadow of the back wall of a store a few seconds later as three men, two armed with shotguns, came running toward him. They stopped almost abreast of him as the hoof drum of ponies abruptly beat out against the silence beyond the bank. One of the trio shouted—"Let 'em have it!"—and swung his shotgun to his shoulder and fired both barrels blindly after Spud and his men. A moment later, as the echoes of the gun blast died to silence, another said: "They got away. Let's look things over." They walked on past Neil Harper.

Alongside the loading platform at the rear of a store farther up the alley, Neil found a partly filled trash barrel and an empty bushel basket. He dumped the contents of the barrel into the basket, set it in place again, and then dropped the money into it. He emptied the trash back into the barrel on top of the money, careful to replace the basket exactly as he had found it. Then, taking off his Stetson, he fanned it along the dust to erase his boot prints.

As the mob collected at the front and rear of the bank, he made his way unnoticed to the far end of the street. Beneath a cottonwood at the rear of a vacant lot near the edge of town he climbed into the roan's saddle and headed out into open country at an easy trot.

III

Barely a half hour after the bank's vault had been blasted open, Spud rode down Bull Fork's main street, left his horse at the feed barn, and sauntered on up the walk to the hotel. On his way he saw the crowd in front of the bank.

At the desk in the hotel lobby he signed the register— **H. Clark, Mesa, Arizona**—and, as he laid down the pen, he asked the clerk: "What's the crowd doin' down the street?"

"You didn't hear about it?" the clerk asked in surprise. He caught Spud's answering shake of the head and went on to explain: "That bunch that raised so much hell in Prairie City last month struck this country today. This mornin' they made a try at the stage and tonight they blew open the vault to the bank. Got away with close onto twenty thousand. The sheriff's out of town, and we're in a hell of a fix."

Spud frowned in concern. "Wonder how long it'll take 'em to work down onto my home range?"

"No tellin'," the clerk said resignedly. He handed across a key. "Your room's fourth to the right along the upstairs hall."

Spud didn't go to the fourth door on the right along the second floor hallway. He stopped at the second on the left and knocked softly on the panel. The light showing through the crack below the door abruptly went out. A few seconds later the door inched open.

Phineas T. Porter said: "So it's you. Come on in."

Spud entered, and closed the door behind him just as Porter struck a match and went to the table to lay his short-barreled .45 on it. He lit the lamp. When the wick was burning evenly, he turned to Spud with a narrow, satisfied smile on his face. "That went off nice, Spud. No one saw you, and from the way the crowd's talkin' you made a good haul. How does it feel to be in the money again?"

A beady perspiration was dampening Spud's narrow brow. He was a trifle pale. "Boss, I hate to tell you this, but we lost every damn' dollar," he said. "Me and Curly and Mel got as far as the door and. . . ." He went on to tell his story in a voice that grated with suppressed anger.

Porter listened with his face gradually assuming a bleakness that once or twice made Spud hesitate to go on. But finally he finished, and after that a long-drawn silence held both men. Spud's glance fell before Porter's hard stare.

Porter said tonelessly: "That's twice in one day, Spud. And four against one both times!"

Spud let a gusty sigh escape from his flat chest. "It looks bad, boss, but there wasn't a thing we could do. He came right up out of nowhere and had that iron of his lined square at us the whole time. I reckon you should have made a try at him when you met him here at the hotel today."

"Don't tell me what I should have done!" Porter flared. "What good would he be doin' us dead and with that payroll money cached where we couldn't find it?" He started pacing up and down in front of the table at the room's center.

Spud let the silence drag out again until it became unbearable to him. "Say the word and we'll go after him tomorrow. This time we'll do the right kind of a job."

Porter wheeled on him. "Can't you get this straight, Spud?" he said in a voice edged with scorn. "This afternoon he was worth ten thousand to us alive. Tonight he's boosted it to thirty thousand." He resumed his pacing once more. "He was smart about it when I warned him about the sheriff. Came right out and the same as told me he was makin' a try at the bank tonight. Maybe he knew I'd try and beat him to it."

Abruptly Porter halted in mid-stride. He turned slowly to

face Spud, and his anger was replaced by a shrewdness in his glance. "So he wants to throw in with us, eh? Told us where to meet him. Spud, we're goin' to frame that jasper! We're goin' to frame him so bad he'll pay every last dime of that thirty thousand to us to get him out of it. And once he's been paid, we'll see how he looks stretched out in a pine coffin."

"How you goin' to do it?"

Phineas T. Porter told him. They parted company an hour later. Neither had a hard time sleeping that night.

At three the next afternoon Spud rode into the bare sandy yard facing the waist-high walls of the ruined adobe house a mile to the west of Bull Forks. He reined his bay close in to the walls and looked inside the enclosure. He saw nothing but the dead ashes of a fire.

Disappointment showed plainly on his face as he put the bay into the shade of the big cottonwood that grew a few rods below the ruin out of the stone foundations of what had at one time been a small spring house. It was a hot day, and he pushed his Stetson onto the back of his head and mopped his forehead with his bandanna. He cursed softly once. A lot depended on his meeting this stranger, and he saw the stranger wasn't here.

"Shed your iron and I'll climb down and we can talk," came a drawling voice from above him.

Whipping his glance upward into the leafy mass overhead, he saw the stranger sitting astride a limb ten feet above. A walnut-handled Colt .38 hung limply from the stranger's hand. There was an indolence in his attitude as he sat with his back to the tree's thick trunk, yet the very ease of his posture held as much of a menace as though his weapon had been pointed at Spud.

"Sure," Spud said, reaching down and unbuckling his

belt. He dropped it onto a thin patch of grass and swung aground on the opposite side of the bay. By the time Neil Harper had climbed down out of the tree, Spud was squatting with his back to the trunk, his hands busy shaping a cigarette.

He handed across the makings. Neil took the Durham sack and built a smoke. After he lit it, he sauntered over to pick up Spud's belt and holstered six-gun. He opened the weapon's loading gate, pushed out the loads, and then handed it across. He smiled thinly as he said: "This'll make it a little more friendly."

"You believe in holdin' all the aces, don't you, stranger?"

"It generally pays." Neil looked at him levelly. "What's on your mind?"

"I'll ask you the same. You said last night there were some jobs you couldn't handle alone. What does my bunch get out of it if we throw in with you?"

"Your bunch?" Neil frowned. "I had you pegged as an understrapper."

Spud decided to let the remark pass. "You're lookin' at the boss," he said.

"You mean, *you're* lookin' at him," Neil corrected. "That is, if you come in with me."

The muscles along Spud's jaw hardened. He let his hard glance run the length of Neil Harper's high-built frame, from the pale blue eyes to the blunt-rowelled spurs on the soft, close-fitting boots. Once again he decided to let a remark pass he would ordinarily have taken exception to. He was remembering Porter's orders.

"Have it your own way," he said. "Only let's get down to business. What can we help you with?"

"Two or three things. One's a bullion stage that rides four guards down out of a boom camp twice a month. It carries close onto fifty thousand a trip. Another's a trail herd headin' north within the next three weeks, feeders to be shipped to the Iowa corn country. There'll be five hundred critters and not too big a crew. I have a market for the whole bunch if we can make a fast two hundred mile drive before the law catches us. And to carry us over the winter I've got title to a ten-section outfit close to a range that's glutted with stock. The hills are close and the sheriff in the next county is blind if you count him in on the split."

Spud whistled softly, forgetting his impassive manner. He admitted inwardly a grudging respect for this stranger.

"I'm to get a third on the split, the rest of you the other two thirds," Neil continued. "You. . . ."

"Hold on!" Spud blared, with a nicely timed show of stubbornness. "We're makin' an even cut or it's no go. Me and my partners have managed pretty well so far on our own."

"Except for yesterday."

"That's another thing. How do we split what you got from the stage and the bank?"

"We don't split it," Neil said. "Your bunch is makin' out all right. You got enough out of that mine safe at Malpais to carry you a while. And you didn't drive that remuda you unloaded from the freight at Prairie City clear to the border for the fun of it."

"That doesn't have a thing to do with this. We're. . . ."

"Take it or leave it," Neil cut in.

Spud glowered up at him, trying to make his hesitation appear natural. "All right," he said finally. "We'll take it. Only, before we throw in with you, there's one deal we have lined up that we're goin' to finish."

"What kind of a deal?"

"Ever hear of Henry Graham?" Spud asked.

Neil nodded, a sense of foreboding striking deeply in him.

"This Graham is worth a couple hundred thousand,"

Spud went on. "Yesterday he was on the stage when we stopped it . . . after you'd emptied the boot. He was fool enough to make a try for his iron. He got a hole through his shoulder, and he's laid up for a few weeks."

Neil said impatiently: "Lay off the wind and tell me what you're tryin' to say."

"This Graham's got a daughter. And it happens that today the daughter is takin' a cattle buyer out from town to her old man's lay-out for a look at some of the old gent's critters. She'll never get there."

In one brief instant Neil Harper's thoughts gyrated uncertainly, and then settled into a clear pattern. He was remembering the girl who had followed the wounded man across the street yesterday from the stage to the doctor's office. One of the men standing on the walk near the stage had told him her name—Betty Graham. For five weeks now Neil had dogged the back trail of this wild bunch, hoping for the chance to be included in it. But he hadn't counted on this unforeseen circumstance. He dreaded Spud's answer as he queried tonelessly: "Why won't she?"

"Because right now two of the bunch are waitin' out along the trail for her and that cattle buyer to come along. They're takin' the girl and maybe measurin' the buyer for a coffin. Tonight Henry Graham will start thinkin' about parting company with ten thousand dollars so he can see his daughter again."

Neil slowly nodded, the set smile on his lean face belying his inner unsteadiness. Abruptly he saw what he must do. He said: "Why only ten? That's one thing you'll have to learn if you're sidin' me. Either go in for big stakes or none at all."

"You think we ought to ask more?" Spud queried, eyeing Neil sharply.

"At last twenty thousand."

"Then it's twenty. Only you don't get in on it."

Neil laughed dryly. "That suits me. It was your idea. Anything I can do to help?"

Spud shrugged his thin shoulders. "Nothin' I can think of, unless you're gettin' tired of your own company and want to hang around camp for a day or two until we wind things up."

As Spud came to his feet, Neil said: "It'll take me about five minutes to catch up my jughead." He nodded down at the weapon at Spud's thigh, adding: "You can put the kick back into that hogleg while I'm gone."

"Thanks," Spud countered dryly.

Forty minutes later they rode to the crest of a low knoll far to the north and looked down into a shallow draw. The smoke of a fire rose lazily beyond a scattered growth of stunted cedars at the bottom of the slope.

Spud whistled shrilly. "We'll wait here," he said.

In half a minute Mel Dewey stepped out of the cedars and trudged toward them up the hill. He was breathing hard from the climb as he approached. He glanced first at Neil then at Spud, and a broad smile came to his coarse features. "Our new partner, eh?" he queried.

Spud nodded. "Take him on down to camp with you, Mel. Did you have any trouble with the girl?"

"Not much. She's got spunk, though. We had to tie her up."

Spud looked across at Neil. "I'm headed for town to see that Henry Graham gets word of this tonight. It might work out better if the girl don't see me. So you still think it ought to be twenty thousand?"

"That'd be my figure," Neil answered.

"Then I'll be on my way," Spud said, wheeling his bay around.

Neil sat watching the gaunt outlaw ride away.

Mel finally said: "Come on down and meet the bunch, stranger. We've got some beans on the fire and a set of healthy appetites. I'm always hungriest just before we make a big haul like this."

He led the way down the hill and toward the fire.

IV

Shortly before dusk that evening Phineas T. Porter drove Henry Graham's buckboard into the far end of the street at a dead run. The blacks were lathered and badly blown. Porter's forehead was gashed and bleeding and his coat and trousers were torn and soiled. Curly had managed to give him this appearance without hurting him much. He swung the team of blacks in at the hitch rail before the jail so suddenly that the buckboard tipped and for a moment threatened to overturn.

As he climbed down from the wheel hub, he let his knees buckle so that he sprawled on his back in the dust. Sheriff Bob Hefflin was one of the three men that ran out from the walk to lift him to his feet. The lawman was quick to see that something serious had happened and growled at his two companions: "Get him inside the first thing! He can talk later."

They took Porter by the arms and steadied him across the walk and into the jail office. Hefflin snapped—"Set him down!"—and, by the time Porter had been eased into the chair, the sheriff had found a half full bottle of whiskey in a drawer of the desk and was offering it. "Take a good nip," he said, handing the bottle to Porter.

The liquor was unaged bourbon and seemed to satisfy Porter. He reached up and wiped the blood from his forehead with the back of a hand. Then, as though suddenly remembering something, he croaked hoarsely: "Sheriff, the Graham girl! He got her!"

Hefflin's look sharpened. "What about Betty Graham?"

"Gone!" Porter said. He felt in one of his coat pockets and drew out a crumpled piece of paper and handed it to the lawman.

Hefflin's face blanched as he read what was written on the paper.

"What is it, Bob?" one of the two onlookers queried.

The sheriff read aloud. "Henry Graham. If you want to see your daughter again, have twenty thousand dollars in tens and twenties and fifties ready tomorrow night . . . Thursday. Send it by a man wearing a white rag tied around his right arm. He is to ride out the trail that leads west from town. He will start from town at nine and come alone." Hefflin looked across at Porter. "It isn't signed."

"It doesn't have to be," Porter told him. "The man you're lookin' for is the one that got out of town ahead of you yesterday, the one that got the payroll."

Hefflin said: "You're sure?"

"Dead sure. He had his face covered, all but the eyes. But it was him. He called me by name. The girl put up a scrap, and I managed to get a hold on his arm while he was tryin' to pull her down out of the buckboard. He gave me this. . . ." Porter touched the gash on his forehead. "Knocked me down in the road and did a good job on me with his spurs."

"Kicked you?"

Porter nodded.

Hefflin's face was set bleakly. "What were you doin' out there with Henry Graham's daughter?"

"Graham and I had a cattle deal on. He was better today, but it didn't look like he'd be up and around soon enough to finish our business before I'm due to leave town. So he sent the girl along with me to go out to his lay-out and look over some stock. This happened about six miles out, right where the trail swings north through those hills. He was forted up in the trees and. . . ."

Hefflin reached out and took Porter by the arm. "Come along to the doctor's and you can tell this to Graham and me at the same time. You ought to have that cut looked after."

At eight thirty that night Spud rode into town. He, too, turned in at the hitch rail in front of the jail. He found Sheriff Hefflin and three others in the jail office.

He asked meekly: "Is the sheriff in?"

Hefflin swung around in his swivel chair. "I'm the sheriff. What can I do for you?"

"I'm not sure you can do anything," Spud said. "But late this afternoon I was on my way back to town from one of the outfits west of here. Six or eight miles out, while I was cuttin' through that line of hills out there, I saw a buckboard comin' toward me, maybe half a mile ahead. There was a man and a woman in it. The woman looked like a girl, only it was too far to tell for sure. Right after I spotted 'em, a man on a roan horse sloped down out of the timber and stopped the rig. I couldn't see all that went on, but I was close enough to tell that the two men were sluggin' at each other. Then this jasper on the roan rode off with the girl."

Hefflin was sitting ramrod straight in his chair. He said quickly: "Go on. What happened then?"

Spud gave an embarrassed smile, let his glance fall. "I'm a stranger here, so at first I thought what I'd seen wasn't any of my business. Then I decided it wouldn't hurt to follow the girl, maybe to be sure she was all right. The roan went along slow since he was packin' double. And when we hit the open stretches, I hung back out of sight and took up his sign." Spud shrugged and once more let that disarming smile again take possession of his face. "As it turned out, it wasn't my business, I reckon. This cowpoke and his girl went north about five miles and made camp. I left 'em buildin' a fire."

The sheriff lunged up out of his chair. "Tripp, go to the hotel and get Porter!" he snapped to one of the listeners.

"Loomis, you get down to Doc Tyler's office and tell Graham I'm takin' a posse out." He wheeled on Spud. "Stranger, can you find the place that killer took the girl?"

"Killer?" Spud echoed blankly.

Hefflin nodded curtly. "I've got a Reward notice in my desk here offering a thousand dollar reward for him. In case you've got a good memory and can find him for us, you get the thousand."

A frown of disbelief gave way to a broad grin on Spud's face. "For a thousand I'd ride from here to Canada," he drawled. "Get your posse together and come along."

Thirty-two riders left town by the west trail twelve minutes later. There had been some delay due to Hefflin's and Doc Tyler's trying to persuade Henry Graham to stay in bed and not ride with the posse, but Graham's blunt remark had been: "I want a good horse and that sawed-off Greener of yours, Hefflin! Leave the rest to me." Even though he had lost a lot of blood not thirty hours ago, Henry Graham managed to get on his clothes and climb into the saddle of a gray gelding from the livery barn. Each succeeding minute, as he and Hefflin led the posse farther from town, seemed to put new strength into him. Once he said: "Bob, I want you to make me a promise. I want the first try at that sidewinder!"

Hefflin nodded mutely, set himself to holding a fast, mile-eating pace. Spud rode alongside him most of the way. Twenty minutes after they had filed down the street he called to the lawmen—"This ought to be the place to cut north."— and swung his bay horse off the trail.

Mel and Curly and Tim proved poor company. They didn't go out of their way to make Neil feel that he wasn't included as one of them, but they did show the average reluctance of range-bred men to accept a stranger.

After they had finished their meal, they asked Neil to sit in at a game of draw poker. He refused on the pretext of having to mend a broken bridle. He sat across the fire from them, ten feet to one side of where the girl lay in the blankets they had arranged for her. They had tied her arms to her sides with a length of rope, for she had fought Curly on the way in and they weren't taking any chances.

Neil replaced a short length of worn rawhide in the roan's braided bridle. As he worked, he was thinking of the girl. Finished with the bridle, he took apart his Colt and cleaned and oiled it. When he assembled it again, he held it in his hand a moment, cold-bloodedly wondering if he could shoot all three of Spud's men before one of them could cut him down. But there was the chance that they would get him first and, thinking of the girl alone with these men, was what finally decided him against taking the chance.

That faint interest she had awakened in him yesterday when he first saw her standing in the stagecoach door had tonight become a strong one. He had seen her refuse to share their evening meal, even refuse a drink of water, and later she had kicked Mel in the shins when he came to ask her if she wanted an extra blanket. Her willfulness and her lack of any sign of fear, along with the biting scorn she showed these men, told Neil of a strength of character lying behind her good looks. She had dark hair, brown eyes, and her face at times was beautiful. It hurt him a little to see the utter contempt in her eyes directed on him the same as it was on those others.

He was thrusting his six-gun back into its holster when Mel Dewey threw down his cards and said: "You two can go blind lookin' at the pasteboards in this light, but I'm turnin' in." He got his blankets and saddle and carried them far outside the narrowing circle of light cast by the dying flames of the fire.

"I'll take a look at the horses," Curly said. As he sauntered out of the light and up the slope beyond which the horses were staked, Tim yawned and looked across at Neil.

"Want to stand watch the first three hours?" he queried.

When he caught Neil's answering nod, he carried his blankets out to where Mel lay and for a few minutes Neil heard the mutter of their voices, and once a hint of sound he couldn't identify, as though a boot had scraped against gravel. Then all was quiet.

Neil looked over at the girl. She was awake and staring at him. He had a sudden thought that made him go over and get his canteen and bring it to her. He smiled as he looked down at her and queried: "Drink?"

He had his back to the fire, yet as she stared up at him it wasn't hard to catch the look of utter contempt in her eyes. She said bitingly: "I suppose you're very proud of this."

Neil thrust a hand in his pocket, the smile vanishing from his face and leaving it completely sober. His hand came out holding his clasp knife. He opened its one long blade, and, with his back turned toward the spot where Tim and Mel lay, he dropped it onto the girl's blankets, close enough so that the handle touched her hand.

First surprise and then amazement edged into her glance. Neil saw her hand strain against the rawhide that bound her arms and her fingers opened and closed on the knife. He asked again: "Sure you won't have some water?"

The smile she gave him made his pulse pound. The contempt had gone from her glance and in its place was an expression of deep gratitude. "I think I will," she said.

He knelt beside her, put an arm about her shoulders, raised her off the blankets, and put the canteen to her lips.

While she drank, he said in a barely audible voice: "Do what you can without moving. Wait until the light of the fire dies down and watch me. We'll have you back home before sunup."

It was while he was holding her, finishing with what he had to say to her, that a gun's throaty explosion beat out across the night's stillness. That sound was from close at hand and must have been a signal, for it was followed immediately by the not distant hoof drum of many running horses.

As Neil wheeled to face the sound of the gun, palming up his Colt swiftly, a gruff voice behind him said: "Throw up your hands!"

It was a strange voice, one he had never heard before. He let the .38 fall from his hand, making out an indistinct shape behind the girl. Then, as the running horses came close in a confused welter of sound, the girl gave a choked cry— "Dad!"—and struggled to a sitting position.

Henry Graham, his left arm in a sling, came into the light. Neil immediately recognized him. Graham said hollowly: "Lie down, Betty. I don't want to hit you when I cut him down!"

"Don't, Dad!" the girl cried. "He was helping me to get away! Here's the knife he gave me."

Graham paused briefly, and that hesitation of his was what probably saved Neil Harper's life. For an instant later Sheriff Hefflin stepped in behind him, rammed a six-gun in his back, and said to the rancher: "I've got him, Henry."

The next two minutes left a pattern of complete confusion in Neil's mind. Countless figures came up out of the darkness to surround him. A few lifted Betty Graham to her feet, cut loose the rawhide about her arms. Someone piled fresh wood onto the fire and the blaze caught and gave them light. A pair of handcuffs was snapped about Neil's wrists.

All at once Sheriff Hefflin was shouting: "The girl says there were three others. Circle and head 'em off!"

A few men ran back into the shadows and a moment later their ponies left the draw at a slogging run.

Above the sound of the moving men, the cursing and their shouts, Neil heard Betty Graham, explaining to her father and the sheriff, whose gun still prodded Neil in the back: "Three of them . . . this man didn't come until later. . . . No, he wasn't the one that stopped the buckboard out on the trail."

Hefflin was all at once shouting: "Porter! Someone get Porter for me! And bring over that lanky jasper that brought us out here!"

Half a minute later Neil was the center of a tight circle of sullen and curious posse men. Phineas T. Porter stood well within that circle. So did Spud Siringo. Seeing the two of them steadied Neil. The hard, uncompromising anger in the eyes of the circle of faces brought the hint of a smile to his sun-blackened face.

Beyond the margins of the group, a mounted rider rode into the light. "They got away, Sheriff," he announced. "There was three of 'em, all right."

"Never mind that, Bob," Henry Graham put in. "I want the straight of this before we string this gent up to that cotton-wood we passed a quarter mile back. Get on with it!"

Hefflin, looking at Porter, asked: "Is this the man that stopped you on the trail this afternoon?"

Porter, scowling, nodded briefly: "I'm ready to swear it was him, Sheriff."

Hefflin muttered an oath under his breath, his look one of perplexity. Ignoring Porter, he faced Spud and queried: "You saw only one man in camp here tonight?"

"Only him." Spud jerked a thumb at Neil. "The others

must have come later. I reckon he's one of the bunch that stuck up the bank last night."

Neil responded: "You'll have to make a better story of it than that, Spud."

"You know this man?" Hefflin barked, staring bleakly at Neil, and then at Spud.

Spud said: "Never saw him before in my life."

"Where the hell's that rope?" Henry Graham growled. Across from him a man tossed over a coil of hemp. With dexterous fingers, Graham shook out the loop and flipped it over Neil's neck.

"Dad, please!" Betty Graham put in. "He was one of them, but he was the only one who offered to help me. Doesn't that count for something?"

"Not with me," Graham said. "Like as not he planned to double-cross the others and collect the money himself! Sheriff, if you don't like what we're goin' to do, we'll excuse you. Tripp, you and Mart and Stouley get over here and grab his arms. Someone bring me a spare horse!"

Neil at once turned to face Hefflin, whose face was flushed and whose manner was one of indecision. "Sheriff," he said. "Reach in my vest and take out the envelope in my pocket." As the sheriff hesitated, he added: "It'll only take you a minute. Graham might like to see it, too."

The lawman reluctantly flipped back the right side of Neil's vest. The corner of a folded envelope stuck out of a pocket. He drew out the envelope that bulged thickly. With one last suspicious glance at Neil he opened the envelope and took the four sheets of paper from it and began reading. Henry Graham grunted curtly—"Watch him, Mart!"—and came to stand alongside Hefflin and read over his shoulder.

Phineas T. Porter's smug smile gradually vanished before a look of puzzlement. He was watching the sheriff's face, which was undergoing a slow change of expression. Henry Graham's grizzled visage was even more changed. His jaw was hanging open in amazement, and once he reached out and snatched a paper from Hefflin's hand to inspect it closely.

Neil was the first to speak. "Maybe you'd better take off these handcuffs," he suggested.

Then, before the bewildered glances of these men, Hefflin took out his key and unlocked Neil's handcuffs, even gave him back his gun that he belted about his waist.

Graham breathed: "This is on the square? You're Neil Harper?"

Neil said: "Look at the picture."

Suddenly Bob Hefflin held up a hand to still the mutterings of the group. "Men, we've made a big mistake somewhere along the line. This man is the detective from the Cattleman's Association we were all yellin' for. He's been here workin' under cover and we didn't. . . ."

"Sheriff, it's obvious that this man's an outlaw and not a detective!" Porter interrupted. "I demand his immediate arrest! Let's finish what we started!"

Above the mutterings of assent, Hefflin held up one of the four sheets of paper in his hand. It was a Reward notice printed in bold-faced type. "Here's a fake dodger put out by the Cattleman's Association. It's got his picture on it. . . ." The lawman was smiling now as he looked at Neil. There was a touch of admiration in his glance. "I've got a letter here from Jim Bodell, a man you all know. Jim says that Harper was sent down here on the toughest assignment ever given a man. He was to get in with this wild bunch, find out who they were operatin' with, and clean out the whole gang."

"And, by God, he's done it!" Henry Graham told them. He turned to Neil. "You've got that payroll hid safe?"

Neil nodded. "That and the money out of the vault at the bank."

Hefflin was incredulous. "This man's saved us something like thirty thousand dollars, gents," he cried, his words coming fast. "Someway he found out what this gang was going to do and beat 'em to it! How the hell he happened to be here tonight, I don't know. But I'll bet my last dollar he can tell. . . ."

Porter moved violently to break in on his words. The man's hand suddenly darted in under his coat and came out fisting a Colt .45. Using it as a club, he whirled and struck down the man behind him. Then, as the others gave way before this unexpected attack, Porter lunged clear of the circle of men and jumped across the fire to whirl and level his weapon.

"Stand back!" he snarled, and the menace behind his words made a few who were going for their guns stop the moves of their hands.

"Watch out, Spud!" Neil warned.

Spud Siringo tried to push back out of the way, out of line with the open lane that had cleared through the circle directly in line with Porter, but the posse men were pressed too thickly about him.

Porter's hawkish face took on a wicked smile. "Comin' along, Spud?" he queried, leaving no doubts in Spud's mind as to what he meant.

Spud saw Porter's six-gun swing around at him. Frantically he clawed the weapon from his thigh. Porter's weapon exploded into the utter stillness. Spud, caught with weapon half drawn from leather, uttered a strangled cry and bent at the waist and went to his knees.

As he fell forward, Neil Harper lunged to one side, clear of the circle of men. His hand streaked down and up from his

218

thigh in an effortless motion that amazed Betty Graham, who was watching him. One moment his hand was empty, relaxed; a split-second later it was lining the .38 hip high.

Porter swung his weapon around and lined it, rock-steady, at Neil. Their guns beat a sharp thunder at the same fraction of a second. Neil's tall frame jerked heavily backward as the double explosion cut loose, but at the same time Porter's right hand twisted sideways and his weapon spun from his hand.

He reached out with his left and caught the .45 in mid-air. But as he frantically thumbed back the hammer, Neil's six-gun spoke again, and again, four explosions so closely timed that they were one prolonged roar cut loose from his weapon. Porter's wide frame jerked spasmodically four times in a broken forward stagger that had the look of defying the slamming lead that was trying to knock him back off his feet.

Then, as the gun thunder died out—while the posse men, paralyzed by surprise and horror, stood motionless—Porter's eyes glazed over, his left hand opened to let the six-gun fall, and he fell heavily face down into the blazing cedar fire, the force of his fall spreading the live coals in a broad circle.

They pulled his lifeless body from the fire. Neil, disgusted at what he had been forced to do, threw his six-gun far to one side. Then, looking bleakly at Hefflin and Henry Graham, he said in a flat voice: "That's how he wanted it, I reckon. Sheriff, the payroll is buried in that cutbank above town where you found the saddle. The bank money is in a trash barrel behind a store up the alley from the bank."

He clamped his hand to his left side where blood was crimsonly splotching his shirt and vest. He turned and started to walk away, but suddenly his knees refused to support him, and he sprawled awkwardly on his face.

★ ★ ★ ★ ★

Later, in Tyler's office in Bull Forks, Bob Hefflin held the lamp while the medico finished bandaging Neil's side. Henry Graham sat, pale and silent, in the deep leather rocker by the door, watching Tyler. Betty stood alongside the chair, her hand on her father's shoulder.

They had been listening to Neil now for five minutes. It was the longest speech he had ever made in his life, yet a necessary one. "There had to be a man working with the bunch," he now said. "Someone who could come to a town ahead of them and line up their jobs . . . someone traveling under a good name and engaged in legitimate business. Up at Ledge I got acquainted with Porter. He was a likeable gent, and I didn't suspect him. But when I came to Prairie City, he was there. That's when I first started to think it was him.

"I happened to meet that gang right after I held up the stage. I found what those four looked like. Later in the day one of 'em came to the hotel to see someone. I didn't know who until Porter warned me that you were lookin' for me, Hefflin. I figured he wouldn't have warned me unless he didn't want me arrested, unless he wanted that payroll worse than he did seein' me in jail. From there on all I needed was proof. And I never got it."

Doc Tyler said: "I'll fill out his death certificate in the mornin'. That's all the proof you'll need."

"Those others'll never come back," Hefflin put in. "They wouldn't be much good without this understrapper that Porter cut down."

Tyler finished his bandaging, straightened, and started rolling down his sleeves.

"How does his side look, Doc?" Henry Graham queried.

"The bullet hit the ribs, glanced," Tyler said. "Nothin' to worry about. He's a damn' sight better than you'll be unless

220

you pile into bed for a week!" Tyler was emphatic. "Henry, you were a fool to go along tonight. You. . . ."

"I wouldn't have missed it for ten years of my life," Graham said, cutting him short. He looked across at Hefflin. "Bob, you still aim to turn in your badge without runnin' next month for reëlection?"

Hefflin nodded. "I'm fifty-eight, Henry, too old for this work. I'll give way to a new man."

Henry Graham had for the past few minutes noticed something about Neil Harper that at first irritated and then pleased him. Harper, in telling them his story, had spoken mostly to Betty. It was as though he was trying to make his excuses to her for what he had done. Graham cast a shrewd glance up at his daughter and caught the light of happiness and pride in her eyes as she looked at this tall stranger. Henry Graham knew the signs.

"So that leaves us without a sheriff," he now muttered. He looked sharply at Neil. "Harper, how much pay are you drawin'?"

"Eighty a month and expenses."

Graham snorted in disgust. "A damn' cheap outfit you're workin' for. The sheriff's job here pays a hundred and a quarter." He waited, watching the change of expression on Neil's face. Then, before Neil could speak, he growled: "Well, will you take it or won't you?" Neil was looking at the girl. Graham understood that look and added: "And if that ain't enough to get married on, we'll boost it a little."

About the Author

Peter Dawson is the *nom de plume* used by Jonathan Hurff Glidden. He was born in Kewanee, Illinois, and was graduated from the University of Illinois with a degree in English literature. In his career as a Western writer he published sixteen Western novels and wrote over one hundred and twenty Western short novels and short stories for the magazine market. From the beginning he was a dedicated craftsman who revised and polished his fiction until it shone as a fine gem. His Peter Dawson novels are noted for their adept plotting, interesting and well-developed characters, their authentically researched historical backgrounds, and his stylistic flair. During the Second World War, Glidden served with the U.S. Strategic and Tactical Air Force in the United Kingdom. Later in 1950 he served for a time as Assistant to Chief of Station in Germany. After the war, his novels were frequently serialized in *The Saturday Evening Post*. Peter Dawson titles such as *Gunsmoke Graze*, *Royal Gorge*, and *Ruler of the Range* are generally conceded to be among his best titles, although he was an extremely consistent writer, and virtually all his fiction has retained its classic stature among readers of all generations. One of Jon Glidden's finest techniques was his ability, after the fashion of Dickens and Tolstoy, to tell his stories via a series of dramatic vignettes which focus on a wide assortment of different characters, all tending to develop their own lives, situations, and predicaments, while at the same time propelling the general plot of the story toward a suspenseful conclusion. He was no less gifted as a master of the short novel and short story. *Dark Riders of Doom* (Five Star Westerns, 1996) was the first collection of his Western short novels and stories to be published. His next Five Star Western will be *Ghost of the Chinook*.